THROUGHOUT ETERNITY

A Romantic Fantasy

by

Lawrence Vincent Stefanile

Quiet Night Publications

ISBN – 13: 9780692559895

ISBN – 10: 0692559892

■

First Edition
December 2015

Chapter One

Now We Are One

Chapel of the Sacred Heart

Capella Del Cuore Sacro

The Outskirts of Naples ~ Italy ~ 1945

"Jersey"

Most of the guys in my squad had nicknames. We called the fastest runner flash, the smartest guy Plato, and the guy with the best pick-up lines Romeo. I have no outstanding attributes; I am just a guy from New Jersey, so my buddies called me Jersey.

I never gave much thought to life's mysteries, or the mystery of my life, for that matter. When I shaved in the morning and looked in the mirror I never reflected on my image as being a one-of-a-kind me or maybe I was a composite of fragments of other past lives. I never thought about the inscrutability of time. I believed time moved inexorably forward. I never thought it might be moving backward or in a never-ending circle or that maybe we mortals are the single thought of a universal mind, replicated beyond human accounting, which toyed and spun us adrift into uncharted streams of time that flowed in all directions into infinity.

Until I reached eighteen, I palled around with my buddies, playing baseball and chasing girls. We loved the Yankees and hated the Red Sox. When we went to Lincoln Park to play we were always the Yankees. It was easy to

1

become Joe DiMaggio, all it took was printing the number five on my tee-shirt with a burnt cork much to the annoyance of my mother. We found empty soda bottles and got enough in returned deposits to admit one guy into the Stanley Theater. When the coast was clear, he'd open the emergency exit door and we'd sneak in before the crack of daylight alerted the usher.

We hung out, across the street of Saint Aloysius Academy, w e c a l l e d i t S n o b H i l l, whistling and commenting loudly on how the girls looked in their uniforms. We wondered where the best looking girls were. One day we counted them into our crude classifications. Soon, we decided all the girls were pretty cute.

As with so many young men, it all changed for me on July 21, 1942. I always thought letters possessed mystical qualities. They express the full range of human emotions, love and loss, hope and fear, rejection and acceptance. They carry thoughts traveling through time and space, and they enjoy a distinct immortality. Once I wrote a letter to the girl of my dreams, but fearing rejection, I never sent it to her, and to this day I don't know what happened to it.

On that day in July, I arrived home from another day of aimless wandering with my buddies. My father and mother stood like statues, they just stared at me. Then my father announced a telegram had come and he pointed to it on the kitchen table. What's in it? I asked.

My father shrugged in an, I don't know attitude. Like pop, mom looked worried. She didn't speak. W h e n I reached for the telegram an oblong panel on the kitchen wall unlatched, and the small ironing board it held crashed down, on my hand. Did you hurt yourself?

I said no, Ma, I'm okay. I pushed back the ironing board, latched the panel and opened the telegram. It said what we knew it would say. Order to Report for Induction, 6:30 AM, City Hall, Grove Street, Jersey City, New Jersey, for training and service in the Army.

Pop crushed me in a powerful bear hug that almost took my breath away. He cuffed my shoulder and then squeezed it with the stevedore strength in his hand. He went outside. I heard him crying. Mom was still stunned. I told her not to worry that everything will be okay. She came to me and quietly buried her face in my chest and closed her eyes. She said, my son, and then she fainted.

For the next two years, like millions of other guys, I tried to survive. I don't know where this story begins or ends, it has many beginnings, but I don't believe it has an ending. It starts in a small church outside Naples, Italy, in the village of my father's birth and early childhood. Fighting in the village had ended with the Germans driven out of their positions and the American infantry in control.

The Chapel of the Sacred Heart ~ *Capella del Cuore Sacro* ~ sat on a gently rising knoll at the far end of the main street in town. I remember it as being a pretty wide street for such a small village. It had a grassy island through its center. It reminded me of Hudson Boulevard that cut across the county from North Bergen to Bayonne.

I visited the church, less to pray, more to feel what pop experienced when he was a boy, to see the bench he sat on during Holy Mass and the altar he knelt at when he took the Communion wafer on his tongue. Pop left for America before his twelfth year. I don't know if he ever made his Confirmation in Italy.

3

The chapel was quiet, the way most chapels are quiet. It smelled of incense. I dipped my powder burnt fingers into the holy water dish. It was dry. Sunlight streamed through broken stained glass windows. It bathed the chapel's Stations of the Cross and mosaics, on its ancient walls and its statuary in a somber fluid-like purplish red tint.

I touched the armrests of each row of benches and thought maybe this is where pop sat during Holy Mass or maybe here or here. I scanned the altar, still intact despite weeks of intensive bombings and fighting. I thought maybe there, that's where pop knelt when he made his First Holy Communion.

I decided to say a prayer, not for me. I learned in two years of combat that survival was a matter of luck. It was as simple as that. American and German soldiers prayed to the same god. I doubted God said, "Today, I'll let the Americans kill the Germans. Tomorrow, I'll let the Germans kill the Americans. Then, I'll think about next week." There is only good luck and bad luck on the battlefield. Then, I thought maybe there are supernatural forces dictating who the lucky and unlucky bastards are.

I would say a prayer for Mom and Pop.

I started up the center aisle to the gleaming white marble gold trimmed altar. A huge statue of the crucified Christ hung on the wall. I looked left and right, and over my shoulder for signs of danger. After all, this wasn't like going to Sunday Mass in New Jersey.

Each step I took split the silence. Silence always seemed strange to me. How could silence be silent when it produces its own sound?

4

A high school teacher answered that question for me. He was one of the few teachers I paid attention to. With a few minutes left in each period he would say, "Okay, let's talk about life." Those were the best minutes of my four years in school.

He had a ruddy face and a neatly trimmed gray beard. Tips of three cigars peeked out of his breast pocket. He spoke in a thick Irish brogue calling the boys, lads, and the girls, lasses. He'd peer over his eyeglasses, particularly at the class clowns, of which I was a charter member, and then he'd say, "Let's talk about silence."

He opened his Khalil Gibran book and began reading.

"Silence illuminates our souls. It whispers to our hearts, and brings them together. Silence separates us from ourselves, makes us sail the firmament of spirit and brings us closer to heaven; it makes us feel that bodies are no more than prisons and the world is a place of exile."

When finished he closed his book and placed it at the center of his desk. The room was quiet, you could hear a pin drop, and we were all caught up in our thoughts.

Then the bell rang.

I left the c l a s s room, but before leaving the building I looked through the door's glass window. He was reading his book and calmly blowing smoke rings that grew larger as they traveled through the air.

On that day, just days from my 18th birthday, I started to grow up. I thought about what he had read. I

5

turned his words over in my mind, realizing the sounds of silence are not in what is said or heard. The sounds of silence are the mystical strains of the true heart.

As I neared the altar rail, I realized my boots weren't the only sounds I heard. There was another soldier in the chapel. I stopped and saw him bless himself with the Sign of the Cross, rise from the kneeler at a small side altar and pick up his rifle. He put on his helmet and turned in my direction. He was a German soldier. The combat instinct in me clicked. I pulled my rifle's trigger. A shot echoed throughout the chapel. The soldier fell backward, onto the marble floor.

I went to see if he was alive. How could I cross, with respect in front of the altar that held the Holy Sacrament? I took plenty of whacks on the back of my head from pop for not showing proper respect. What would I say after genuflecting and blessing myself?

"Dear Lord I just shot a man in your holy house, and probably killed him, amen."

I threaded among the assembled benches and got to the small side altar where the German soldier had prayed.

I saw he was no longer a danger to me. His rifle was out of his reach. He was on his back breathing softly. He raised an inviting hand to me. From days of bombing small tiles from the Sacred Heart of Jesus mosaic on the wall above were falling to the marble floor and dancing around him. The bouncing chips reminded me of the dice games we played to kill time while we waited. It seemed we were always waiting.

The soldier tapped his chest and motioned to me for help. I unbuttoned his breast pocket and removed from it an envelope and a picture. I looked down at the dying soldier. He was about my age. I could have been his negative. He had blond hair and blue eyes. I have black hair and brown eyes.

I held his envelope and picture before his eyes. "Do you want me to mail this?" I asked. He shook his head yes and said in German, in a fading voice, which oddly, I understood, "The letter, please, mail to my wife. The picture, you keep."

He brushed his fingers across his wife's name on the envelope. I looked at his picture. It was beautiful. I had the feeling I was in the life of its scenery. The soldier pointed to the bottom of the picture to where he had signed his name, and then he tapped his chest.

With ebbing strength, he said, "I am artist." In that moment my combat instincts deserted me. I took his hand. I looked up at the crucified Christ and cursed the war. The soldier squeezed my hand and whispered; "Now we are one." Then his hand slid from mine. He closed his eyes and began his journey into eternity.

I took his letter to my platoon sergeant. I asked if he could get it to the soldier's wife. He looked at the envelope, and then he looked at me.

"It's addressed to Dresden, Jersey," he said.

"Yeah," I said. "So what?"

"The British fire bombed Dresden. Dresden has been incinerated. Even if she's alive it will never get to her," he said, a trace of sadness in his voice. "What do you want me to do with it?" he asked, chewing on his cigar.

7

"What would happen if I don't take it?" I asked.

"We're fighting a war, Jersey we're not the post office. It will die here like her soldier died in the chapel."

I killed the guy, and I couldn't even keep my promise to him. I was tortured by the intensity of my failure. I hated this goddamned war, the senselessness of it all.

Dusk descended and the rumble of artillery faded. The clamor of combat disappeared. Suddenly, it was quiet. I thought of my high school teacher and his leather-bound book. In my mind, I saw him, plain as day, peering over his glasses, his beard bobbing up and down to the rhythm of his words, reading to us from his treasured book.

"I'll take the letter."

He asked what I was going to do with it.

"I don't know; maybe, I'll find her, and tell her how her husband died in the chapel."

"Ya' seeking forgiveness, Jersey?"

"I don't know," I answered.

He handed me the letter.

"I guess we all need forgiveness," he said and walked away.

I went outside. The war for me was over. Before going home I went to Dresden, the city where so many died. I found the street written on the soldier's envelope. I weaved through smoldering ruins. I saw ribbons of smoke boiling out of bomb-mangled streets. I felt heat on the soles of my feet. Although destruction was everywhere, I saw where the soldier's inspiration came from; the glinting river, the canopy of blue sky, trees in autumnal colors in the fall and crystalline snowflakes in winter's star-studded nights.

She couldn't have survived the firestorm.

I flashed back to another day in class and heard again his Irish brogue.

"The river flows to infinity," reverberated in my head.

I placed the soldier's letter on the river's tide.

Chapter Two

Warm Smiles through Cold Glass

Jersey

Pier 51 ~ New York City ~ Home ~ Jersey City

1945

I arrived at Pier 51, on the Queen Mary, in New York City, on a sunny day in June, 1945. Most of the guys lined its decks as the ship eased into its berth. They returned waves to the swelling crowd, their eyes searched for wives, children, girlfriends, mothers, fathers, grandfathers, and grandmothers. Everybody buzzed nervously, awaiting the piper's shrill notes that would unleash a torrent of humanity, home safe from the war. I remember this guy, on spotting his wife holding high their baby for him to see, and a small boy hanging on her skirt, clutched the deck's railing, and fell to his knees crying. People carried homemade-signs with all kinds of messages. A young woman, pretty cute, as I remember, waved her sign, side-to-side like a metronome. It read, *Darling! I'm Yours!* Comments crackled up and down the deck. Most of the guys claimed the young woman for themselves.

"Hey, that's my girl!" they yelled above the din.

The piper blew his whistle and the exodus of thousands of guys started. Within seconds, the pier was a crucible of raw emotion. It was the biggest love festival I had ever seen; strangers clung to each other, kissing, hugging and crying or bravely trying to hold back tears.

There were enough tears shed to float another Queen Mary. Love, leavened with sadness, blossomed all over the pier. Men and women met for the first time. In an instant they knew, as only people whose lives are lived on the edge of agonizing moments know, they would leave the pier as friends destined to become lovers.

Mom and pop weren't in the crowd. My embarkation orders had been screwed up. I wrote and told them I would see them when I got home. I didn't join the rush down the disembarkation ramp. I had a cup of coffee and smoked a Lucky Strike and waited until the line thinned out.

As the ship and pier emptied, save for the river lapping against the dock, calm came to the pier. It was strange; one minute, raucously gleeful, a carnival of human emotions, and the next, quiet introspection. Lives that had touched lives on a sunny day in New York City would go separate ways, parting forever, to relive this day in gauzy memories in old age. A serene quiet descended, as if a mystical historian had come from some ethereal place to record a grand celebration in the shadow of a majestic ship, moored on a great river.

I disembarked with a handful of guys. We acknowledged one another with nods and indecipherable smiles. Then we went our separate ways. I took a last look at the Queen Mary. As I left the pier dock workers shook my hand and grabbed me in bear hugs. The older men fought back tears; I knew they were for their lost sons.

"Hey! GI! Where are you going?" a soldier with three stripes on his sleeves, standing next to an Army jeep, hollered to me from across the street.

Jersey City!"

"Come on!" he waved to me.

"Hop in. I'm going to Fort Dix. I'll drop you off on Journal Square."

I got in. He floored the accelerator and the jeep took off. He was a smooth driver, probably drove the brass. We cruised through the gloomy Holland Tunnel. When I was a kid, I rode through the tube into Manhattan with Pop. His truck was loaded with merchandise destined for the ship lines along the river. I remember looking at Pop's barrel chest and his powerful arms sculpted by years of hard work and the expert way he shifted and drove the rig under his command. Back then, I thought pop was indestructible, but years in combat changed me, forever; I now know no one is indestructible, not even pop.

In a short time the glare of daylight flooded the jeep and we arrived at Journal Square. We shook hands and wished each other luck. I watched him speed away. I never saw him, again.

It seemed strange to me as if I was on a turntable looking around at the familiar harbors of my youth. Then it hit me. I was home. I looked to my right, at the Stanley Theater. I pictured my buddies sneaking through the emergency exit I had opened. Now they are gone; one buried in France, the other buried in Italy. They'll never grow old; in my memory they will be forever young. What would I say to their parents? Would they hold a grudge against me for surviving the war when their sons didn't make it?

I walked past the theaters and stores that dotted the street. An elderly woman stopped and kissed me. She said nothing and continued on her way. I walked down the hill past the firehouse, on my way home.

I recalled balmy summer nights when pop and I walked up the hill, to the newsboy, and pop bought a *New York News* and a *Daily Mirror.* Before going home we stopped in the drug store for cherry cokes.

It seemed I couldn't get home fast enough. I walked past houses with gold star and blue star flags in their windows. The faster I walked the more out of reach home seemed to be. It was like some of the girls I dated. The harder I chased them, the more distant they seemed until the teasing ended and I caught up. I stopped to catch my breath.

When I got home the door was unlocked. I left my duffel bag in the hallway and climbed the five steps inside. It was as if the years hadn't passed. I looked at pop at the kitchen table drinking coffee, smoking his Old Gold cigarette and tapping its ashes into the saucer. Mom was at the window, pinning sheets, shirts and pillowcases to the clothesline and sailing them across the yard.

The sounds of home reminded me of what I had missed, laundry snapping in the breeze, spoons stirred in coffee cups, mom's soft humming. I hoped to hear once again, in the safety of my room, the whisper of rainfall across my bedroom window in the night. I watched mom and pop's quiet devotion tears streaming down my face.

I tried to sleep in the quiet of hot summer nights, without artillery thundering in my head. Sleep didn't come easily, and all too often, not at all. I called some of the girls I had dated before the war; most of them were married, engaged or had moved away. I went with pop to the corner tavern. I never paid for a drink. On the far wall of the tavern the owner had hung framed uniformed portraits of the neighborhood guys serving in the war.

Each portrait was arranged across the wall in a pattern that spelled VICTORY.

When I was alone at the wall a strange silence came over the tavern as if an invisible acoustical veil had been strung along its center. On one side, I heard the usual sounds of men talking at a bar, on the opposite side, at the VICTORY wall, a deafening silence. I looked at my portrait and wondered if I had ever been that young. I touched the frames of the portraits on the wall and only got warm smiles through cold glass in return.

The tavern owner had placed black ribbons in the frames' right hand corners of the guys who did not come back. Pop said, each time he did, he cried and went to a back room to compose himself. I came to the portraits of my two buddies. I wanted to relive memories with them, but I couldn't, words wouldn't come. I touched their faces and felt only cool glass. I left the tavern to visit with their parents.

Before leaving, I looked back at the old timers at the bar. If I get to be an old man, I'll remember them, chattering at a bar and portraits of young men, smiling at them.

I took my GI Bill and enrolled in the night division of a local college. I got a job with the Greenville Railroad at its Greenville Station. After filling out the new employee papers I shook hands with the yard manager. He said my first assignment was to inventory files stored in a shack scheduled for demolition, many of which were over a hundred years old. He said it was a tedious job and promised me summer help.

We left his office and went outside. The hot sun on my freshly shaved skin was invigorating. The yard manager handed me a key. He pointed a small shack standing wearily in the shadow of a giant willow tree. He said that's where the files were stored.

I jerked to a sudden plume of black smoke that blew into the air. I was home, but a part of me was still in Europe. I felt the yard manager's reassuring pat on my shoulder. He said it was the firebox cleaning out coal from the steam engines. They were called blackouts. He told me the railroad notified the women on Willow Street each time a blackout was planned so they could take in their washed laundry. Alerting the women to the blackouts was a part of my job. With a wry smile, he confided how one day he forgot to notify them and an army of angry women cornered him. Laughingly, he said, if they had their way it would be him, and not their laundry hanging from their clothes lines. He shook his head side-to-side. His mouth curled in a smile. He lit a cigar, exhaled a wreath of smoke into the air and went inside.

I walked past the roundhouse where a steam engine was being shunted into another direction by a turntable that emitted yawning metallic groans. The constant movement of engines and railway cars produced choruses of screeching, steam belching noises that banged around in my head.

I crossed over parallel and crisscrossed rail tracks, to the shack. It was ancient and sooty from thousands of blackouts. I unlocked the padlock and pushed open the door. Dust threads danced in the beam of sunlight that shot into the room. I slapped my hand on a stack of files and watched dust threads fly into the air. I felt like a kid, again.

The room was crammed with files. Some were stacked at eye level. A metal frame cot sagged beneath the weight of boxes piled on it. I organized the files in rows, according to years. Some went back to 1845.

After several hours, the stifling heat in the shack sapped my energy. I should have gone outside for fresh air. Instead, I sat on the cot and looked at the sea of files. The cot was strangely familiar. I felt as if I were in my room, at home. I kept an old Phillies cigar box under my bed. It contained the secrets of my youth. From time to time I'd look into the box, at old newspaper clippings of Yankee box scores, a photograph of me and my two boyhood friends, and a letter I had written to the girl I had fallen in love with. I never mailed it to her. When I came back from the war I looked her up, but she had moved away; nobody knew where to. I looked for my letter in the cigar box, everything was there, but the letter had disappeared. I never found it. I guessed I would never see her again.

In combat, I lived on the edge of mortality. It sharpened my awareness and helped me survive. Now that I was home I hoped my state of agitation would abate and the flashbacks would disappear, but they never did.

I don't know what intuition guided me to reach under the cot. I pulled out a battered sack imprinted Vollmer Farmhouse. Out of respect for its age, I carefully took from it a music box with figurines of a dancing couple and an envelope browned with time.

I removed a crumbling letter, dated March 13, 1864. In its fold were a pencil sketch and a pink ribbon.

I held the letter to the sunlight and began reading.

16

Chapter Three

Sign of the Cross

A Battlefield in Virginia

Early Spring ~ 1865

"Vollmer! Will Vollmer! Where the hell is Vollmer?"

"I'm comin', Sarge," Will elbowed through a crush of Confederate soldiers.

"Ya' here like clockwork when there's no mail for ya'," Sarge growled. "Now!" he waved an envelope above his head, " I can't find ya' when ya' got mail."

"Sorry, Sarge."

"Here ya' go, lad," Sarge offered the envelope to Will; abruptly, he retracted it.

"What's wrong?"

"Nothin'," solemnly, Sarge made the Sign of the Cross over the envelope and placed it into Will's outstretched waiting hand.

"What's goin' on?" Will' s words drowned, as if caught in a riptide. He saw Sarge decomposing, dissolving into the ether, disappearing into nothingness.

17

Then Will snapped awake; his heart beat like a drum and his head clanged like a cathedral bell. It was the same recurring dream; night-after-night, for the past year. Its inexplicability shook Will to his core and scared the hell out of him.

Combat does strange things to men, shooting surreal images in and out of their minds, twisting thoughts, like taffy molded into a sticky mess at the County Fair.

If Will's dream had any meaning he couldn't find it. So he dismissed it thinking some of the guys see themselves as dead, that way nothing matters, and fear can't sink its claws into them.

Through an opening of stacked sycamore logs that fortified the defensive line Will surveyed the sprawling green field before him where he discerned vague movements of the Union Army preparing the assault he knew was soon to come.

"We all want to be somewhere else, where death's not nipping at our heels. Seeing ya'self as dead is one way of getting through it all. All of us have our own ways of puttin' up with the horrors," Will ruminated.

Will took a picture he had sketched from his haversack. He looked at it longingly. With a smile he affirmed the hope and beauty he saw in it, and then referentially returned it to a secure place.

A mounted rider on a black Arabian horse with a distinctive white rose on his forehead thundered past. He tossed a mail pouch that hung in the air before it fell to the ground in a burst of dust.

Without breaking stride the rider galloped past Will and disappeared around the fortification that poked into the road like a sore thumb.

It had been a long time since Will's unit had a mail call. A rasp of Sarge's command brought soldiers to him, like pollinating bees flying to a rose bush.

In his thick Irish brogue, Sarge called names off envelopes in his hand. When no one came forward, he made the Sign of the Cross over them, muttered, *"Requiescat in Pace,"* and placed them at the back of the pack in his hand.

The soldiers idolized their cigar-chomping sergeant. They said he had the heart of a lion and the soul of a poet. His blue eyes twinkled beneath thick shaggy white brows. He wore his ever-present garrison cap at a crooked angle fighting any man who tried to remove it. A large silver cross of the crucified Christ dangled indifferently from a chain around his neck. Sarge was fearless in battle and compassionate in its aftermath. He called the soldiers in his unit his lads.

The buzz in the ranks had Sarge a defrocked priest from Ireland, whose affair with a young Irish nun resulted in her pregnancy. They came to America and settled in Boston. When mother and child died in child-birth, Sarge was inconsolable. He sought solitude and left Massachusetts for the life of a farmer in Georgia.

"Vollmer! Will Vollmer! Where the hell is Vollmer?"

"I'm comin', Sarge," Will elbowed through a crush of soldiers.

"Ya' here like clockwork when there's no mail for ya', Vollmer," Sarge growled. "Now!" he waved an envelope above his head, " I can't find ya' when ya' got mail."

"Sorry, Sarge."

"It's happening," Will thought. The dream is becoming reality; Sarge delivering mail; the men around me; Sarge calling my name, three times. Will shuddered. "It doesn't mean anything", he rationalized. "It was only a dream."

"Here ya' go, lad," Sarge offered an envelope to Will; then, abruptly, he retracted it.

"What's wrong?" Will said.

"Nothin'!" Sarge retorted.

A surreal stillness gripped the soldiers. Sarge removed his cigar from his mouth. He looked into Will's eyes. With the solemnity of a priest giving Last Rites, he made the Sign of the Cross over the envelope and placed it into Will's outstretched hand.

Will walked the somber corridor of fellow soldiers clutching his letter, looking at the men, all bowing their heads in sorrow to avoid staring at him.

At the sycamore fortification Will opened the envelope and began reading his letter. Suddenly, he stopped, numb and unmoving. In those d a r k moments nothing mattered.

Then he felt Sarge's arm around his shoulder.

"I know, lad," he said, "I know. You must go back to your post."

Will looked with vacant eyes at Sarge, unable to speak, incapable of grasping the reality of his letter's contents.

"Come, lad," Sarge repeated, tugging him to his post. "Come," he said, again, in a low voice.

Will collapsed against the rude logs of the defensive fortification. He stared with unseeing anguished eyes, his sensibilities anesthetized.

"Your life has purpose, lad," Sarge whispered, and then, he vanished.

In those brief moments, each endowed with its own eternal dimension, Will knew his life would be lived in two parts; the briefest was the happiest filled with joy and future promise, and now that was gone, an unrecoverable illusion, and if he survived the war, Will knew his life would be lived in days of endless loneliness.

Chapter Four

Counting Fireflies

Greenville, New Jersey

New Year Day ~ Early Morning ~ 1900

A freezing wind howled through boxcar corridors in a bleak railroad yard in Greenville, New Jersey. The sky was alight with fireworks celebrating New Year Day. On his rounds of the yard Will heard Mary's telepathic holiday greeting. Although long departed, Mary was irreplaceable to Will. She was always in his imagination reliving memories and comforting him through his lonely days and interminable nights.

"It would be a happier New Year if you were here with me, Mary," Will answered, turning up the wick in a rusted lantern that illuminated his way through shadowy corridors of sullen boxcars, jiggling their locks and closing shut open doors.

"I know you do. I miss you, too, Mary. It seems each passing year brings me closer to you."

"It's 1900 here; unlike your address we mortals still count time," Will laughed. "It's uneasy going into a new century; they say strange things happen at the start of new centuries, I guess I'll see for myself."

Will winced to a boom of fireworks that flashed in the sky.

"You are such a worrier, Mary always fussing over me," Will startled to another boom.

"After all this time I still can't get used to sudden noises."

"I'm all right," Will countered Mary's concern and quickly added, "On second thought keep it up; when you fuss, I feel I could reach out and touch you," Will smiled.

Successive displays of fireworks brightened the night. Streamers, the colors of the rainbow fell, languidly from above, and then slowly, the sky faded to blackness

"It's beautiful, Mary. I'm glad you saw it. The streamers remind me of the pink ribbons you wore in your hair, and the yellow roses you tended in your garden. The booms didn't startle me that time. I'm getting better."

A sudden spasm erupted in Will's chest wracking his sides and spewing metallic tasting sputum into his mouth. Within minutes his coughing subsided and his shuddering body calmed.

"It's just a cough. It will go away. We southern boys aren't used to northern winters. I know you're worried. Promise me you'll try not to worry. I'll be fine," Will said, on his lonely rounds of the railroad yard.

"It's snowing, Mary. It's not like the warm nights we knew in Georgia."

"Remember that wonderful June night, rocking back and forth on the porch swing, your head on my shoulder. I still feel your sweet breath on my face.

Will became quiet. He heard only the sounds of his roiling lungs, and his crunching steps on the snow-covered gravel paths.

"Sorry, Mary," Will apologized for his silent interlude. "You know I get this way every so often. I want always to remember, but remembering is sometimes painful. I think of that June night as if it happened yesterday. We counted fireflies in the distant field. Then you said there were too many winking at us. We sat for hours. I kissed you. You kissed me back. And then you laced your fingers in mine. Do you remember what you said?"

"Yes, I remember," Mary's telepathic voice articulated in Will's mind, "I said now we are forever."

"Listen to the crickets and you put your head against my chest. Even in a night this cold I still feel the warmth of your face and the scent of your hair," Will said, wistfully.

"You said the crickets were serenading us and closed your eyes and pressed yourself close to me. I loved the sound of your soft breathing. I couldn't hold you tight enough. I couldn't get enough of you. I felt time stood still that there was no tomorrow and the way we were that night would never end. It's like yesterday, just like yesterday," Will repeated his emotions trapped in his throat.

Will ratcheted up the lantern's fading flame. He turned into a blast of icy wind on his way to a shack beneath an over-arching willow tree that had been his home for four decades.

"The willow is so sad in wintertime," Mary's thought transference articulated in Will's mind. "In the spring it is green. I hear music singing in it. You look so peaceful sitting in its shade. I wish I could be with you, to smile with you and to laugh with you as we did so long ago."

"I go there to relive our wonderful days."

"I treasure those moments; they are part of my eternity," Mary communicated.

"I can't describe the feeling that comes over me when I am there," Will said, "It's as if I've escaped this unwanted reality and gone back to the world we both love. You are always in my heart, Mary."

Then Will felt a breeze on his face, like a kiss. He looked up, into the falling snow and threw his kiss heavenward.

Will crossed over the snow-encrusted railroad tracks that crisscrossed the yard. He squeezed between snow-caked boxcars before coming to a side path. Only the lantern's burning wick illuminated his way through the snowy night.

"There you go, again, Mary. Don't worry, I'll be warm tonight. The army came through with a shipment of horses. I inspected the boxcars with the captain in charge. The horses were magnificent. I'll never forget one. He was an Arabian, black and powerful with a white rose on his forehead and soulful eyes. The captain left a stack of blankets. He said they wouldn't be needed where he was going. They smell like stables, but they're heavy and warm," Will said, before his voice trailed off.

Will swung his lantern side-to-side to a steam engine lumbering around a bend of tracks through the gathering snow and sinking temperatures. Its engineer acknowledged with a rhythmic toot-toot of his whistle.

In the distance the willow tree was barely discernible. Will lowered his head into the blasting wind and headed home.

Chapter Five

Snow Flurries in the Sun

Greenville Railroad Yard ~ New Jersey

New Year Day ~ Early Morning ~ 1900

Will lay on his cot his eyes glued to the splintered ceiling low above him as if it were an archive of his life's story. He remembered the long ago night when he came to the railroad yard leaving forever the south, but not his haunting personal and battlefield memories.

Back then Will had no idea where his northern trek would take him. Along the way he learned the railroad yard in Greenville, New Jersey, was to be his destination, and his destiny. The shack, which was to be his home, was new and strong then. Now, at the start of a New Year, and a New Century it was old and weary, its face stained with ash and coal dust, its once strong foundation frail, its demeanor one of resignation.

Will mirrored the shack he lived in for four decades. His room was somber and lonely. A single kerosene lamp its sole source of illumination. The sack under Will's cot, worn from years of opening and closing, removing and returning its contents was all that remained of any emotional connection to his world. In it were a music box, a letter, a pink ribbon and a sketch. He had read the letter thousands of times until it began crumbling in his hands.

27

Will fought to stay awake, not for the exhilaration of a New Year and a New Century, only for Mary, to continue their comforting telepathic communication, until sleep possessed him.

"Guess what today is?" A suppressed cough followed Will's quiet laugh. "I know its New Year day. You always know how to wind me up," his ardent feeling transferred to Mary through the incalculable distance of their worlds. Then Will drifted into a reflective mood.

"You came to us fifty years ago, today," Will said. "Lately, everything seems like it happened yesterday. It's as if I could reach back and touch that day. Time evaporates like snow flurries in the sun," Will suppressed another spasm of coughing.

"I wish you could have seen snow, Mary. You would have loved a snowy day."

"The world is quiet when snow falls. I hear only the peaceful sounds of silence. I wish we could have walked together in the snow and you could have felt frosty flakes on your face. How I wish we could have done all that," Will said, closing his eyes to ease the pain of his unrealized desires.

"In a few hours, I'll go to the other side of the yard, to check the boxcars; some are as big as our farmhouse, many are waiting to leave the yard."

Then Will became silent.

"Good night for now, my love," he whispered, turning down the lamp light. In the darkness muted shadows danced on the peeling walls of the small shack. Will closed his eyes and fell into a deep sleep.

Chapter Six

Her Joy Was Limitless

The Vollmer Farmhouse

Greenville ~ Georgia

New Year Day ~ 1850

In the early morning of January 1, 1850, a small girl sat on the front porch of the Vollmer farmhouse in Greenville, Georgia. She cradled a doll in her arms. She smoothed its hair, straightened its cap and remarked with a dimpled smile how pretty the doll's blue eyes are. She sang a child's lullaby pausing every so often to look about, and then returning her attention to the doll in her arms, she resumed her soft singing.

A green field stretched before the farmhouse where the small girl sat. It inclined gently and at its crest merged with a clear blue sky. Behind the farmhouse an iron fence encircled the family burial plot where a single white headstone stood in the shadow of a peach orchard patiently awaiting the gifts of spring.

Mother Vollmer welcomed the peaceful quiet of the early morning of the first day of the New Year. She wore her dark hair to her shoulders tied with a pink ribbon. Her brown eyes were warm and thoughtful, like her nature. She busied herself in the kitchen preparing a surprise breakfast for Father Vollmer and Will.

New Year days had always made Mother Vollmer reflective. She recalled her good memories; comforting memories when her family was whole and its future bright. Then there were memories that deeply wounded her, memories she couldn't dismiss, no matter how hard she tried.

She recalled the moments of Will's birth.

"You have a son, Father," she said, cradling the small boy in her arms. "Are you pleased?"

"More than you will ever know, Mother," he responded kissing her gently. Since that day their pet names, Father and Mother, stuck.

"It seems as though everything stops on the first day of a New Year. It's as if the planet stops spinning," Mother Vollmer tied an apron around her waist. "People are like the planet," she thought, setting out rolls and butter, bacon and eggs and jams and jellies. "The planet never stops spinning on its journey into infinity. We humans go round-and-round, and then our journeys end; we don't know when or what our eternal destinies will be."

She looked through the fogged kitchen window, at a small headstone in the family plot. It read, *Baby Girl Vollmer, 1845*. In days gone by Mother Vollmer stood statue-like at the kitchen window for hours staring at the white headstone wishing the infant buried there to resurrect, wishing so intensely her head throbbed and her heart raced as quiet tears rolled down her face.

"Your journey was too short, my baby girl. You must know," placing her hand over her heart, "Your mother carries you here and she always will."

In the dream that drove her into a state of deep despair the bedroom is dark and the midwife and Father Vollmer are quiet. Their faces are pale, their joyous expectations supplanted with shock.

The expectant cries of a newly born baby girl filled Mother Vollmer's mind. Her joy was limitless. She took the baby from the midwife and pressed her to her breasts. But her baby girl was not alive. The cries that filled Mother Vollmer's nights were her desolation, her imprisonment from which she could find no escape.

Mother Vollmer despaired at the loss of her baby girl. Her vibrancy, once the light of her family now lay in the ruins of her irreparable loss. She wandered numbly in a labyrinth of confusion finding no exit into the sunlit life she once knew.

As she prepared her surprise breakfast, Mother Vollmer recalled Father Vollmer's patience and solicitude, and she marveled at y o u n g Will's understanding of her pain a n d helping her out of the fog of despondency.

Mother Vollmer had much to celebrate this New Year day. She had returned emotionally to the husband and son she loved most in the world.

Chapter Seven

Someone on the Porch

The Vollmer Farmhouse

Greenville, Georgia

New Year Day ~ 1850

The sizzle of frying bacon and rolls hot in the oven was better than any wake-up call for Father Vollmer and Will. In the kitchen, Mother Vollmer heard their curious stirrings. In a lilting voice, she said, "Be seated gentlemen, breakfast will be served, soon."

New Year Day, 1850 was all Mother Vollmer could hope for. She laughed when Will, now seven years of age asked for his first taste of coffee.

"Will," she smiled, "I have never seen such a funny face."

"It's bitter I like milk better."

"You'll get used to it, son," Father Vollmer said, "Isn't that so, Mother?"

"Will should decide for himself."

"Your mother is right."

"Papa, it seems mother is always right." The three burst into spontaneous laughter.

After breakfast Mother Vollmer cleaned the kitchen. She accepted Father Vollmer's and Will's compliments of her culinary skills.

Father Vollmer asked Will to join him, on his inspection of the farm.

Seeing Will's excitement Mother Vollmer gave her blessing.

"Dress warm, Will. It's chilly outside," she advised.

"The boy will be warm enough," Father Vollmer said. "Let's go, son."

"Haven't you two forgotten something?"

Will giggled at a gentle poke to his side, and he covered his mouth to suppress his laughter.

"Well!" Mother Vollmer exclaimed, her hands on her hips a note of mock exasperation in her voice.

"You go first," Father Vollmer whispered.

Will hesitated.

Mother Vollmer pulled Will to her and kissed him several times.

"Be careful!" Mother Vollmer ordered.

"Happy New Year, dear."

Father Vollmer cupped Mother Vollmer's face in his coarsened hands and kissed her, gently. "I love you very much," he said, softly.

Will opened the front door. Daylight streamed, inside. He watched his father and mother locked in their good-bye, impatient to leave the house and experience his passage from boyhood into young manhood.

"Papa's good-byes with mama always take so long," he mused swinging the door back and forth. Will blinked into the glare of the January sun. He was surprised to see a small girl rocking back and forth, singing sweetly to a doll she cradled in her arms.

He watched transfixed as the girl stood up and came to him. Her eyes were violet and her hair the color of autumn. In future years, Will understood the enchantment he felt on the farmhouse porch that New Year day in 1850.

"I'm going to help papa in the barn."

"It's over there," he pointed, beyond the farmhouse. "Do you want to see it?" The girl shook her head, affirmatively and they went to the far side of the porch.

"I'm going to help with the horses, too."

"See my doll," the girl held up her soldier boy doll.

"Do you want to play with him?"

The girl's doll chilled Will.

"I don't want to play with your doll," he answered, belligerently.

The girl pressed her doll to her chest, to console it.

"Where is your mama?" Will asked.

The girl pointed to the farmhouse.

Will followed the sweep of her arm.

"Your mama isn't in there; my mama and papa are in there."

"She's in there," the girl insisted.

"No, she's not!"

"Yes, she is!" the girl argued.

"Who are you talking to, Will?" Mother Vollmer's voice came through the open door.

"Someone on the porch."

Chapter Eight

An Empty Rocking Chair

The Vollmer Farmhouse

New Year Day ~ 1850

"A visitor on New Year day," Father Vollmer muttered, quizzically. "Who could it be?" Mother Vollmer said, easing herself out of Father Vollmer's embrace.

"Ask our visitor to come in, Will," she added.

The small girl had followed Will inside. She stood in the sun bathed foyer protectively cradling her doll in her arms. Her presence commanded everyone's attention. Mother and Father Vollmer smiled reassuringly prompting the girl to hand Mother Vollmer her doll.

"What a nice doll," Mother Vollmer said. "A handsome soldier boy," she continued.

"What is your name, dear?" she asked softly.

"Mary."

Father Vollmer and Will watched Mother Vollmer with growing interest. She turned to Mary and said, "Mary is a pretty name for a pretty girl."

"Where have you come from?" Mother Vollmer asked.

"I don't know," Mary responded.

"Who brought you here?" Mother Vollmer inquired.

"I don't know," Mary answered.

"Were you outside a long time?"

Mary shook her head, affirmatively.

"Are you cold?" Mother Vollmer asked.

Mary nodded yes, and pressed her face into the hollow of Mother Vollmer's hand.

"Good Lord, you are chilled to the bone!"

"I'll warm some milk," Father Vollmer said on his way to the kitchen.

"Will, bring me the blanket on the sofa," Mother Vollmer ordered.

"We'll get a warm bath going. Mary will welcome one. Don't you agree, Will?"

"Yes, Papa."

Mother Vollmer settled with Mary into a rocking chair next to the parlor's glowing fireplace. She pulled Will's blanket about them and pressed Mary close to her. She hummed softly to the rhythmic swaying of the chair.

With each shudder Mother Vollmer pressed Mary tighter against her body.

Father Vollmer and Will emptied buckets of boiling water into a metal tub both conscious not to dispel the silence that pervaded the household's early morning. Mother Vollmer rocked easily, oblivious to everything, but the girl in her arms.

The empty rocking chair was a constant reminder of Mother Vollmer's loss. Whenever a sudden breeze moved it, Mother Vollmer withdrew into herself. The pain she felt in the past now evaporated at the sight and feel of Mary in her arms.

"Thank you, dear," Mother Vollmer said taking the cup of warm milk from Father Vollmer.

"The tub will cool to a warm bath," he said.

Mother Vollmer smiled, and then quickly refocused her attention on Mary. Father Vollmer kissed her forehead in an understanding of her undivided emotional investment in Mary.

"Will and I are going outside; will you be all right?"

"We will be fine," she said, her eyes riveted on Mary.

"Will is eager to get going," Father Vollmer said, "I'll look in on you later," he added parenthetically.

"I love you both, very much," Mother Vollmer looked away from Mary to Father Vollmer and Will, her voice cracking.

"I love you, too," Father Vollmer said.

Will stood to Father Vollmer's side, his eyes fixed on Mary.

"Let's go," Father Vollmer put his arm around Will's shoulders.

Mary sipped the warm milk Mother Vollmer held to her lips, and after a brief struggle, she fell asleep.

Mother Vollmer kissed Mary's cheeks, and she thought of what might have been.

Chapter Nine

You are Irreplaceable

The Vollmer Farmhouse

Greenville ~ Georgia

New Year Day ~ 1850

The stillness in the Vollmer farmhouse fueled memories that were comforting, but oftentimes disquieting. The tub in the kitchen had cooled to a warm bath. Mary slept peacefully on the parlor sofa.

Father Vollmer and Will worked the farm. The prospect that earlier elevated Will's spirit with the knowledge he was about to embark u p on his journey into young manhood raised his spirits.

Through the kitchen's misted window Mother Vollmer gazed at her baby girl's resting place. The peach orchard had been a source of comfort throughout her days of emotional turmoil. Its cyclic rhythm symbolized the promise of rebirth, and the hope that life was eternal.

Mother Vollmer needed to know that any happiness Mary might bring her would never diminish her love for her lost baby girl. She looked a long time at the white headstone before burying her face in her trembling hands. In the confessional silence of her mind, Mother Vollmer spoke to her baby girl.

40

"A small girl came to us today, my darling. She is five years old your age, had you lived. Her name is Mary. I see your image in her eyes. She does not know how she came to us," Mother Vollmer paused to compose herself.

"How I miss you," her voice cracked. "My heart that beat next to your heart is empty without you. I don't know why you had to leave us. I don't know why you were taken from us before your first light of day. I tried to keep you here, but I failed. I can only hope you have forgiven me; the hurt never goes away, you are irreplaceable.

Before continuing a soft breeze kissed Mother Vollmer's face; it was angelic and reassuring beyond human description. And then, a sudden wind lifted a solitary leaf off a tree branch in the orchard. It came to rest on the white headstone before blowing away in a comforting breeze.

A sense of peacefulness enveloped Mother Vollmer. Wiping tears from her eyes she sensed a stirring behind her and turned to Mary, her arms outstretched.

Mother Vollmer lowered Mary into the tub's warm water. She glistened in the suds and giggled when Mother Vollmer put soap bubbles on the tip of her nose and washed between her toes.

Throughout Mary's bath she and Mother Vollmer exchanged glances; one a child's curiosity, the other, a maternal desire seeking fulfillment.

The bath finished, Mother Vollmer lifted Mary from the tub and wrapped her in a warm towel.

"Now, you are all new."

Chapter Ten

Faceless People

The Vollmer Farmhouse

Greenville, Georgia

New Year Day ~ 1850

In the crook of her arm Mother Vollmer carried a wicker basket stuffed with laundered napkins and towels. She walked past the living room where Mary and Will sat, quietly on the sofa. She relished the scene she hadn't dared to dream; her son and daughter playing contentedly in a peaceful winter's day.

Earlier, Mother Vollmer had dressed Mary in a crisply pressed dress. She kissed her cheeks, tied a pink ribbon in her hair and lifted Mary onto the sofa, next to Will where she sat singing, to her soldier boy doll.

Mother Vollmer smiled at Will's sideways glances at Mary. Will was the delight of her life, affectionate, sensitive and mature, beyond his years. She saw in him the onset of young manhood; his eyes clear and blue like a spring sky and his slender body growing taller and stronger with each passing day. It was difficult for Mother Vollmer to contain her joy. She knew her undisguised feelings were apparent to Father Vollmer, and was aware of the questions that demanded resolution.

Father Vollmer sat preoccupied at the kitchen

table watching the swirling coffee in his cup as if seeking guidance from an Oracle. Mother Vollmer sat across from him, her eyes averted arranging laundry in neat stacks. Father Vollmer continued stirring his spoon in his cup. Mother Vollmer looked up at the clinking sound; th e y smiled guardedly, neither able to pierce the wall of silence that separated them.

Father Vollmer had seen the incandescence in his wife's eyes, the radiant rushes in her movements and the song in her voice that hadn't been there since the stillborn birth of their daughter. His mind and heart told him she had made an irrevocable decision to keep Mary and raise her as their daughter and no force on earth could dissuade her.

From the first day in the small drafty schoolhouse of their youth, Father Vollmer knew Mother Vollmer would one day be his wife. He remembered leaning forward at his desk whispering in her ear, "When we grow up I'm going to marry you and make all your dreams come true." They snickered when their teacher sternly warned, "No talking, children!"

Father Vollmer knew the law required Mary be reported as a missing child, and he knew in so doing, Mary would be taken away. Mother Vollmer continued folding and stacking her laundry on the table as Father Vollmer searched his mind for a way to begin the discussion both knew had to come.

"Shall I go to the Orphans Court tomorrow?" Father Vollmer finally broke the excruciating silence.

"Why must you go to the Orphans Court?" Mother

Vollmer answered, her eyes cast down.

Father Vollmer didn't respond.

"Why must you go to the Orphans Court?" she repeated, testily.

"The law requires a missing child be reported," Father Vollmer said, aware his answer might not be well received. The joy Mother Vollmer had felt since Mary's coming began drowning in a sea of complications. She continued arranging her laundry and didn't speak.

"Are you angry with me?" Father Vollmer asked, after an agonizing pause.

"I don't know what to think. Why can't we be left alone?" Mother Vollmer broke her silence.

"It's the way things are; we have no control, I wish we did. I would never cause you harm; you must know that. If Mary's fate with our family is inhospitable I would be shattered to think you would hold me culpable."

"Mary is not missing!" Mother Vollmer retorted, an uncharacteristic sharpness in her voice. "If she is not missing there is no court with jurisdiction over her!" She swept her arm to the sofa where Will and Mary sat. "She is in the living room sitting on the sofa with our son."

Mother Vollmer rose to her full height, her face reddened in anger at an uncaring system that would blindly dash her hopes and dreams.

"Tell me! How can you or anyone say Mary is missing," she pointed, again, to the sofa. "Tell me," her anger displaced by a sense of exhaustion.

"You must know what I mean," Father Vollmer responded.

"I don't know what you mean!" Mother Vollmer answered.

"Who makes such laws that suit only their narrow needs? Who makes these laws that would deprive a small child of a happy home and not care that the child is swallowed up in some cold, uncaring place? Who are these faceless people who know nothing of our lives and pass these laws only to gratify themselves at our expense?" Mother Vollmer demanded to know tears streaming down her face, her voice trembling.

"I have no answers for you," Father Vollmer said in a barely audible voice.

After a short pause, he asked, "Should someone come forward with a valid claim to Mary, what would you do?"

The question stunned Mother Vollmer. For a time, she was unable to speak. She looked at Father Vollmer. The glare in her eyes faded to a bitter uncertainty. Father Vollmer looked away not wanting to see the pain he knew she was feeling. The mental image of strangers taking Mary from her was unbearable. Mother Vollmer felt her chest tighten and her head spin.

The possibility of losing Mary drained her strength. She stood up and buried her face in her hands swaying back and forth before collapsing onto her chair, her body convulsing in breathless sobs.

Father Vollmer got up to go to Mother Vollmer. Instead, he went to the kitchen window. He looked long at the small white headstone in the family burial plot. He gazed at the peach orchard, its trees cold and gray, its bleak branches pleading for spring and the birth of flowers. He closed his eyes trying to fathom the deep silence of his mind, to gain access to answers that had mercurially eluded his consciousness. He hoped for a message that would show a way out of their emotional wilderness.

Mother Vollmer struggled to bear what might be the loss of Mary. The question of his relationship with Mother Vollmer burned within Father Vollmer. He saw the change in her since Mary's unexplained arrival in the early morning hours. In his heart, Father Vollmer knew beyond any question, Mother Vollmer's consuming desire to keep Mary and to raise her as she would have raised her own daughter.

The prospect of a broken trust and a compromised love haunted Father Vollmer. Would she forgive him if he insisted on handing Mary to the authorities? What would their lives be like? "It's in my hands," he ruminated, repeating, again, "It's in my hands." Father Vollmer knew with the certainty of his own mortality that sundering their love and trust was unthinkable.

A simmering dispute between Will and Mary erupted into crossfire of accusations and counter-accusations. They climbed down from the sofa and raced to the kitchen where Father Vollmer and Mother Vollmer sat at the kitchen table in excruciating silence.

Will and Mary had designated Mother Vollmer the arbiter of their dispute. In an instant, the kitchen became a family appeals court, where Will and Mary sought to obtain favorable verdicts from Mother Vollmer.

"What is this all about, children?" Mother Vollmer demanded. Will and Mary's squabbling continued in rising volume and aggrieved intensities. At Mother Vollmer's intercession Will and Mary calmed, and then just as quickly, they resumed their crossfire.

Mary launched her appeal first pointing an accusatory finger at Will.

"I said he could play with my doll, but he won't play with me. It's my doll, he can play with it, but he can't keep it."

Mother Vollmer looked at Mary's doll. It was the first time she had examined it closely. Its strong resemblance to Will surprised her, and the doll's military uniform was unsettling. In a fleeting moment, she felt there was something prophetic about Mary's cherished doll.

"She always wants to play. I don't want to play with her, she won't leave me alone," Will countered Mary's argument gaining Mother Vollmer's attention.

Reinforcing his argument, Will turned to Mary and said, "I don't want to play with you. Anyway, what is a girl doing with a soldier doll? Soldier dolls are for boys."

"It's my doll," Mary contested. "I love my doll. I'll never let you play with it," Mary shot back.

"I don't care," Will returned fire. "I don't want your doll."

47

"See!" Mary alleged speaking to Mother Vollmer, like a diminutive lawyer confidently making her case, seeking redress of Will's slight.

"Both of you stop!" Mother Vollmer said firmly. For the briefest of moments, Will and Mary stopped arguing, but in a split second, they started up, again.

"She started it," Will defended.

"He started it," Mary retorted.

"I don't like girls with pink ribbons in their hair."

"I don't like you," Mary shot back.

"I don't want to be your brother," Will parried.

"I don't want to be your sister," Mary snapped.

Mother Vollmer looked like a scorekeeper. Her head swung back and forth at each insult, like an official at a tennis match. She tried to contain her laughter.

"Stop your squabbling!" she said, a stern note in her voice, and I mean, right now!"

With darting cross looks the noisy wrangling wound down and quiet returned to the Vollmer farmhouse.

"No more funny looks"

Will and Mary stood before Mother Vollmer. In remorseful silence they answered, yes. At their sudden repentance Mother Vollmer began laughing. She covered her mouth to maintain the seriousness of the situation.

Father Vollmer smiled at the sight of Will and Mary, chastened, their eyes cast down awaiting a verdict that would underscore the righteousness of their claims.

He suppressed a laugh, at Mother Vollmer's cheerful discomfort. "This is only a small taste of what she's in for," he mused.

Father Vollmer acknowledged Mother Vollmer's elation with a smile. Then he became distant. He stared out the window at the small white headstone lonely in winter's chill.

Mother Vollmer turned to Will and Mary and was about to speak when she felt a tug on her dress. Mother Vollmer bent down to Mary who had lifted, on tiptoes.

"Are you going to be my mama?"

Mother Vollmer stepped back; speechless. She brushed Mary's and Will's faces. She knew she wanted to say yes, and live the moment forever in her memory.

She looked to Father Vollmer hopeful of his assent, but his back was to her, hunched at the window staring through the cold glass at baby girl's headstone.

Mother Vollmer turned to Will and Mary, their expectant eyes glued to her saddened face.

In that moment, she felt Father Vollmer's hand on her shoulder, and she looked up.

"Our son and daughter are waiting for their mother's verdict," Father Vollmer whispered.

Chapter Eleven

Confusion and Fear

Greenville Railroad Yard ~ Winter 1900

The Vollmer Farmhouse ~ Winters ~ 1850 and 1862

Wind howled through the Greenville railroad yard. It rattled Will's shack and jarred him out of his sleep. He didn't light his lamp preferring the inky night, finding in the decades since the war more light in darkness than in the brightest spring days.

In time the winds abated, but Will couldn't get back to sleep. He lay awake remembering New Year day, 1850, trying to relive his happier times talking quietly to himself.

"Mother was bursting with joy. Father tried to calm her, but he was unsuccessful. Mother gathered Mary and me to her as if we were flowers in her garden. She kissed father's hand, on her shoulder. She kissed Mary and me, again and again, until we complained. Mother and father were crying. Those were treasured moments, but as with all such moments they are soon gone, leaving behind only fragile illusions.

After lifetimes of conforming to authority mother and father had no remorse ignoring the laws of the state and the county when it came to Mary. There were anxious times when carriages stopped and their drivers looked at the farmhouse before rolling away and unexpected visits of strangers seeking directions.

Father and mother were certain Mary had come to our family by some divine plan. Each day they looked through newspapers for any news of Mary; they found nothing and no one came to claim her.

Mother always believed Mary came to us, where she was meant to be. Life on the farm was pleasant. I wish I could go back to those times. I still see father's and mother's happy smiles; they are always in my memory.

For Mary and me everything changed on New Year day, 1862, Mary's seventeenth birthday. I never thought of Mary as my sister. As the years passed, Mary grew more and more beautiful; she looked lovely in the birthday dress mother had sewn for her. Her excitement showed in the blush in her cheeks that matched the pink ribbon in her hair; the pink ribbon I teased her about when we were children.

Mother presented Mary with a silk handkerchief and father gave Mary a book of poetry. Mary jumped from her chair and hugged and kissed father and mother.

Kings and queens, princes and princesses, couldn't live more enjoyable lives than we did on our small farm in the years before the war.

I had planned Mary's present long before her birthday. Mother and father knew what I was up to, but they kept my secret. The summer before Mary's birthday I collected Cherokee Roses from mother's garden and pressed them in the family bible. I cut a square out of an old barn door. When the flowers dried, I arranged and sealed them on the cutout board. I made a border so the flowers looked like they were in a picture frame. I wanted to make Mary's birthday gift special.

"I have something for you, Mary," I stammered.

"Oh, Will! You are such a good brother!" Mary answered.

I was sure in that moment, as I had known in the months and years before, brother to Mary was not what I wanted to be and I hoped Mary felt the same way. I rounded the table and handed her my birthday gift. What seemed a lifetime she just stared at it and then Mary looked at me, the way I had hoped she would, the way a woman looks at a man.

"It is beautiful, Will," she said, in a barely audible voice. I remember how quiet the room had become and the puzzled expressions on father's and mother's faces. Mary said again, how beautiful my gift was. She kissed my cheek and when she did I saw in her eyes a mixture of confusion and fear.

Mary's face flushed scarlet. She backed away from me, the way a person retreats from a perceived threat. Mother and father looked at each other trying to figure out what they had witnessed. Mary took my gift and ran up the stairs into her room and closed its door, behind her.
We heard her crying.

"Should you see what is troubling Mary," father asked mother

"No, father," mother smiled.

"I know what's troubling Mary."

Chapter Twelve

Thunder Shook the Sky

The Vollmer Farm
Greenville ~ Georgia
Summer ~ 1863

Mary was like a frolicking child running happily through a field of glistening green grass, heavy with early morning dew, spinning like a ballerina her face and hands lifted to the lemon colored sun that rose brightly in a cloudless blue sky.

She pointed to a giant willow tree; its green leaves cascaded from high above. It stood like a citadel beside a foaming silvery stream in a field carpeted with wildflowers of all conceivable colors all swaying drunkenly in the early morning breeze.

"It is a magnificent tree."

"Why haven't we seen it before now, Will?"

"We have come here so many times and until now, we never saw this beautiful tree."

"It's a miracle, Mary," Will said, still amazed at the willow tree's grandeur.

"Let's go," he said, and taking Mary's hand they ran up an inclining slope through a field of wildflowers to the willow tree in awe of it grace and power. They touched its flourishing foliage, the tips of its leaves dipping into the burbling steam.

"Isn't it grand, Will?" Mary said, looking at the soaring willow that reached high into the sky.

"It is," Will said, his eyes scaling the willow's arching branches, up to its crown.

"It is so graceful, Will!" Mary exclaimed. "Look at how it sways even in the gentlest breeze."

"Listen, Mary, the willow is speaking to us. It's inviting us inside."

"There, Will!" Mary pointed to an opening in the willow. "Its branches have parted, inviting us inside," she said, excitedly.

Will took Mary's hand and felt its delicate smallness. He looked into her eyes and smiled. Mary smiled back. They went through the willow's opening as if they were entering their own cottage.

Inside, the willow was cool and quiet, humming softly in easy breezes. Will and Mary surveyed its cupola, its long tumbling branches, the greenish rays that streamed through its leafy pores and the massive trunk at its center.

"Is it not enchanting? Will."

"It's magical, Mary."

Will scanned the willow's architecture and wondered if its breathtaking beauty could have happened by accident or by the will of an unseen power, incomprehensible to the human mind.

"It is our secret place, Will. Here, we will find only peace and happiness. I close my eyes and see our future, our home and Will Jr.," Mary said, flushed with excitement. "You can see it, too, Will. Do you not see it?" Mary asked, seating herself on the cool ground looking up at Will, breathless with excitement.

"I see it," Will said, gently stroking Mary's face. "I see it," he repeated, softly.

Then a howling wind shook the willow shrieking and felling branches beside the stream replacing the willow's gentle crooning with mournful sighs.

Mary's cheeks earlier crimsoned with excitement now paled at the strange feeling that consumed her. She eased herself to the ground her eyes clouded in fear, her excitement now supplanted with dark forebodings.

As suddenly as it arose, the wind subsided, the willow calmed and its mournful sighing stopped. Will eased himself beside Mary and kissed her. Tenderly, he stroked her face, still pale and cold.

"Why are you frightened?"

Mary turned to Will and smiled. She pressed her mouth to Will's hand. "I don't know," she answered. "A strange feeling came over me, it frightened me. I want it to go away and never come back."

"We are safe here, there is nothing to fear," Will pressed Mary closer to him and smiled reassuringly. Mary smiled back a pink flush returned to her cheeks.

"Promise me you won't be afraid, Mary."

"I am afraid to be so happy," Mary said. "I fear something will turn our happiness to dust. We are so happy now. I want it to always be this way. Have you ever felt that way, Will?"

"Let's hope these moments last forever," Will believed what he said and he hoped Mary would shed her fears.

But, the war had come to the Vollmer family.

Mary couldn't accept Will's conscription into the Confederate Army. Night after night she dreamed of her soldier boy doll coming to life. He held her hand and smiled and kissed her, and then an invisible force tore them apart, each disappearing into opposite distant corners forever hidden from each other.

"The world is such a terrifying place," Mary lamented. "This war is taking you from me. What happened to our happy years? Soon, they are gone, leaving only memories. Can't we just stay here and be happy? I'm not asking for much, Will. Life is so short. I'm not asking for much, am I?

Why must there be war? We're told it preserves the way we live, but it doesn't, it changes everything. Our lives are over, before we have had a chance to begin. We're safe here, Will. Let the world go on without us."

"If only it were in my power," Will whispered.

Mary pressed Will's lips with her fingers realizing what she desired was beyond his power. In a lowered voice, she said, "I have loved you from that New Year Day on the porch. I remember, as if it were yesterday."

"You were such a small girl then, Mary, a brat," Will smiled, "I went outside and there you were, with your soldier boy doll, smoothing its hair, rocking it back and forth, and singing to it."

"My doll," Mary interjected, "My eternal guide to you."

"How could you have known then, you loved me?" Will asked.

"You were slow to figure it out. You put it together on my birthday. We saw it in each other's eyes.

"I took my time," Will smiled.

"You took your time," Mary closed and opened her eyes. "The true heart overrules time. I know that, now," Mary whispered. "We have loved each other, forever," Mary turned to Will, her eyes clouded in sorrow.

"We found each other and our love blossomed on earth," Will pointed to streaming light coming through the willow. "I didn't start loving you on that New Year day I have loved you before time," Will whispered.

"But will our love last forever even when our time here on earth is over?"

"Don't burden yourself with such thoughts, Mary."

"Will our love survive death? Will our love go on when all has turned to dust?"

"Wherever we might be, whoever we might be, we will know each other, and we will love each other as we love each other, now."

57

"Throughout eternity, will we be as we are now?' I want to be as we are now."

"As we are now," Will squeezed Mary's hand and kissed her tear streaked face and her mouth, devotedly.

Mary was quiet in Will's embrace. She felt her heart beating against his chest. She wouldn't think of tomorrows; they didn't exist for her, only the present mattered. She knew her moments with Will, in the heart of their enchanted willow to be timeless.

Mary reached up and lightly brushed Will's smooth skin. He pressed her hand against his face and kissed her palm, and then wove his fingers into curls that had escaped their pink ribbon bond. Will pressed his lips to Mary's mouth, lingering on their softness. He breathed in the sweetness of her breath professing his wish that these were forever moments.

Then Mary emerged from a deep sleep.

"Where did we go, Will?"

"I don't know," Will said leaning back, an equally ecstatic look on his face. "Wherever we were, it was wonderful."

"It was beautiful, Will. I felt I was air, itself. I saw all the colors of the rainbow and colors I can't even describe. I saw flowers and butterflies and green mountains and blue streams. I wish I could express how happy I feel."

"I know," Will whispered, "It was a peaceful world; a world without suffering."

"Take me there, again, kiss me, Will, I know your kiss will take me back to that wonderful place."

Will cupped Mary's face in his hands and looked for what seemed an eternity into her eyes, now shining in excitement and passion. His mouth found Mary's soft lips and rested there in long, exploratory kisses.

Mary closed her eyes and she and Will drifted into a transcendent sleep to a special place beyond the stars. When Mary woke she smiled at Will, still asleep his head on her chest.

"Will," Mary whispered.

"Love me, Will," Mary's voice deepened in desire.

"Love me, Will, now, and for all our eternities.

Will looked long into the violet eyes of the small girl who enchanted him, long ago. He kissed Mary's face and mouth, softly, quietly, his eyes glazed with tears.

In those moments, Will knew Mary was the very dawn of his life. He unbuttoned her collar and slid out its pink ribbon.

"You will always be in my heart, Mary."

In the bosom of their enchanted willow, Will and Mary gifted each other their innocence.

While outside, clouds darkened, rain beat down, and thunder shook the sky.

Chapter Thirteen

Only Illusions Remained

Dearest Will

Greenville Railroad Yard ~ Winter ~ 1900

A Virginia Battlefield ~ Spring ~ 1865

In the darkness Will anguished over his lost years, and the life he and Mary could have shared. He recalled cigar-chomping Sarge's last words on that fateful April day, the day Mother Vollmer's letter caught up to him, its contents shattering his life.

"That was the day I died," Will murmured. "Without Mary, I have no life. What purpose does a lifeless man have in this world? Tell me, Sarge!" Will, berated between coughing spells. "What's the purpose you promised, Sarge? When will I know why I exist in this empty shell?"

Will perceived an oscillation in the stillness of his room. He wondered if delirium had played tricks with his mind. A scent of roses filled his nostrils. He heard rustling sounds. The matches he fumbled for slipped out of his hand and he fell back, onto his cot, breathless and consumed with fever.

"Mary!" he called out.

Will felt a touch on his face; it was soft and reassuring.

Then Mary's voice came to him. "I am here, Will. It breaks my heart to see you agonize through these long years. Time passes callously slow when there is pain and all too quickly when there is happiness."

"I knew you would come to me."

"When there is pain time can be cruel. Where I am there is no time, there is no pain. Millions of years are a blink of the eye. When we are together again, it will be as if we were never apart. Soon your purpose on earth will be realized, and then we will be together, in that beautiful place we went to, on that wonderful spring day."

Then the oscillating waves stopped and the room became still. Will fell into a fitful sleep and dreamed of that long ago day on a Virginia battlefield when he sat back against stacked sycamore logs staring vacantly into space. He had read Mother Vollmer's letter, over and over, each time denying its contents, unable to grasp its reality.

13 March 1864
Greenville, Georgia

Dearest Will,

I am writing this letter from our kitchen table as night closes in. I pray my letter gets to you. It will be my final act on this earth. Our small family was so happy, and life on our farm, was so good, for so many years. Those years passed, too quickly.

All is shattered. My heart is broken. Your beautiful Mary succumbed to the fever, as did her baby. Mary gave birth to your beautiful baby boy. She named him Will Jr. Then the fever struck. Today, in the early afternoon, Will Jr. passed away. Then Mary followed. Mary said Will Jr. went first to guide her into heaven. Mary's last words were for you.

61

Mary was a darling little girl. I saw, right from the start you two loved each other. I wish we could have had more happy years. I am grateful for the time we had together.

My fever worsened throughout the day. At dusk, father went outside for water. I heard a musket shot. I went outside to the well where father lay dead. A young Union soldier from New Jersey fell to his knees. He shed anguished tears. He carried father into the house and placed him on our bed.

The soldier didn't want to leave us. He said an order had been given to burn everything. He placed Will Jr. on Mary's chest and wrapped them in a blanket. He buried Mary and Will Jr. in the family plot in the shade of the peach orchard, next to our lost baby girl.

The soldier prepared a place for father and me, to rest beside each other. Then I went to our bed to be with father, until my time came, which I knew to be only moments away. I asked the soldier to post my letter to you after burying father and me. He agreed and then he wept and begged my forgiveness. I held him and I forgave him.

When you think of bygone days think of the love we had for one another. It is love that survives everything. When you read this letter we will all be gone. We will be wherever you look. A day will come, dearest Will when we will all be together, again, in joyous reunion, free of suffering.

All my love.

Your mother

In a mind-numbing day, Will lost all that mattered most to him. The knowledge that Mary had given birth to his son elicited a sad smile that vanished in the certainty of their deaths. He crumbled Mother Vollmer's letter in his hand wanting to be rid of its unwanted contents.

With each passing minute Will's trauma worsened, inflicting irreparable wounds deep into his psyche. His head spun like an out-of-control carousel. He wanted to cry out to the heavens, to berate and question God for permitting the destruction of his family. Primal sounds fulminated in his throat, and finally, desperately, he stuffed his fist into his mouth to stifle the volcanic scream of desolation that erupted within him.

"I'm sorry, mother," Will repeated, over-and-over, weeping, smoothing the crinkled letter, brushing its script, certain he felt the warmth of her hand.

"I thought there would be something to come home to, but there's nothing left," Will mumbled.

"What's the use," he lamented tearing his sketch from his pad. He lingered on the image in his hand, smiling nostalgically at the memories it evoked. Then he placed the sketch in the letter's fold and put the envelope in his pocket and threw away his sketching pad.

Blinded by his catastrophic losses Will didn't care. Men and machines seemed to move in blurred patterns with neither quickness nor conviction. In the sky, Will saw birds in flight seemingly frozen in place their wings immobilized as if affixed with lead weights.

Will perceived the soldiers as soulless fixtures enveloping gray space moving in silent flows, stretching in all directions devoid of individuality their identities obscured in the recesses of their hearts.

The noise of grinding wheels and shouting soldiers came to Will as far away echoes. His thoughts of home stuck in his conflicting desire to remember the happy times and forget the pain of his tragic losses.

The memory of Mother Vollmer's birthday, shortly after Mary's arrival formed in Will's memory. He remembered her opening father's gift, a music box with carved figurines of a dancing couple on its turntable. With the turn of its spring the music box played a gay waltz and its figurines whirled round-and-round to its melody. He recalled how its happy sight and sounds lifted everyone's spirit. Then the spring wound down and the dancing couple and the music stopped playing.

Mary clapped her hands her face flushed with excitement. She asked Father Vollmer to bring the music and dancing back. He turned the spring key and music filled the farmhouse on Mother Vollmer's birthday.

"Who are these faceless people who make laws to satisfy their own narrow needs at our expense?" Will recalled Mother Vollmer's question.

Now he knew what she meant; its meaning rang with a clarity Will hadn't known. He was sure in secret places the unseen hands of faceless people wind the springs of human events. He sensed a time would come when other faceless people conspiring in secret hideaways would wind springs that would reduce the planet to a burnt cinder screaming through apathetic space.

"They are all gone; Mary and our son, father and mother, only illusions remain." For Will, everything continued out of focus, soldiers moved zombie-like their words dripping mournfully from their lips.

Their voices sounded to Will as hollow echoes, as if coming from unreachable obsidian caverns. It seemed to Will the world was dying.

Across the dusty road two soldiers sat, one bearded and older, the other, a boy with porcelain smooth skin that a razor had yet to touch.

The song the older soldier sang in his husky baritone was nostalgic, a plea for the life he had left behind.

Will closed his eyes and listened.

"An exile from home, splendor dazzles in vain,
Oh, give me my lowly thatched cottage again;
The birds singing gaily, they come at my call;
Give me them, with peace of mind, dearer than all."

The younger soldier put down his letter and listened, and then he returned to his writing.

Then the older soldier sang another song. A deep fatalism floated on its notes. The younger soldier stopped writing. He closed his eyes to think no more, to savor the solitude of nothingness he saw in his closed lids.

"Just before the battle, mother,
I am thinking most of you,
While upon the field we're watching
with the enemy in view."

The older soldier's singing plunged Will into a deeper despair. He remembered the sweetness of his Georgia home and how he and Mary planned to marry in the first spring of his arrival home from the war in the shade of the blossoming peach orchard. He remembered his desire to shed his warrior's cloak and become a farmer once again wanting neither a king's treasure nor a prince's estate, only the fulfillment of being a good husband and father. He despaired at the reality of his irrevocable loss.

Will questioned why he lived when all he cared about was forever gone, anguishing into which chamber of his mind to consign his guilt.

Chapter Fourteen

Artillery Serenade

The Final Battle ~ Day One

Sunrise ~ Sunset

Virginia, Spring ~ 1865

The day of the final battle dawned clear and cool. A surreal silence enveloped the Confederate defensive line where soldiers confronted their mortalities; some fatalistic, others bargaining for more time, and y e t others blithely unconcerned.

Will's reflexes were still mired coming in dull unconnected flashes. Barely, he discerned the whining cannon-shot that crashed into the two soldiers across the dusty path. His eyelids lifted heavily, as if breaking a viscous bond at the blast's culminating roar.

In the explosion Will saw the two soldiers rise in the air then return to earth in contorted death poses. The older soldier's musical plea for home forever ended. The younger soldier's unfinished letter stayed with him in the hand of his separated arm, and then it blew away in the wind of the artillery blast.

In the far distance Will saw an orchestral succession of smoke rising in endless recitation along the Union battle line. He heard the artillery serenade of cannon-shot, ripping into men and machine, belching its vaporous blue mist through the defensive line.

Will apprehended all about him to be moving, as if asynchronous with the revolving planet. The shrieking sounds of relentless artillery came to his ears as a progression of exhausted yawns. He heard drowning choruses of screams and bugle calls. He saw soldiers ripped out of trenches hanging listlessly over tree timbers, like torn tapestries.

Will's mind recorded in playback a soldier, disdainfully shaking his fist in the face of booming artillery blasts before he was swept away in the wind of its cyclonic roar. He saw himself trapped in a forbidden cavern ruled over by leering potentates rolling dice on the outcome of the battle, from which Will saw no escape.

Union artillery intensified throughout the day, obliterating fortifications and the men manning them, decapitating treetops, splintering tree trunks, gouging craters into once quiet woods and streams, rocking the field to its geological core.

Will clawed the earth until his fingers turned purple. He cleaved against shattered timbers and covered his ears, to block out endless concussive explosions. He felt his brain lose its power of human thought. He didn't pray throughout the long hours of ear-splitting bombardment; instead, he hoped, and if hope is prayer, then Will prayed for an end to his nightmare.

At dusk dwindling artillery fire echoed long in the valley of Will's mind as he labored out of his fetal position, his brain breathing off its day long instillation of fear. Will looked at the littered dead appalled by their deaths, while strangely envying their surcease from pain and suffering.

An image of the fist-shaking soldier flashed, again, before Will's eyes, wondering if he had elected to end his life or had lost his mind. He wondered if he had the defiant soldier's courage to curse the salivating war beast and end the misery it had brought to his life.

Chapter Fifteen

The Colonel and the Arabian

Good Man! Good Man!

The Final Battle ~ Day Two

Virginia, Spring ~ 1865

A dead soldier slid off a fortification log like a boy sliding down from a tree he had climbed. In detached silence the soldiers resumed their watch for the attack they knew was soon to come.

The acrid bluish vapor of the day-long artillery burned away in the rising sun. In his dream, Mother Vollmer appeared to Will and told him of her lonely quest to heal a void deep in her soul. Before he cried out to her, she vanished and Will snapped awake. He looked heavenward at a ring of birds sailing in a circle, over the battlefield. Then one-by-one the birds flew away and the ring dissolved.

Will scanned the twisting battle line past soldiers in lifeless poses where they had fallen as if a master puppeteer cut his marionettes' strings. He thought again about the defiant soldier trying to decipher the forces that drove him to certain death.

In the artillery lull a high-ranking officer cantered along the dusty road that separated the defensive line from the woods. He saddled a charcoal-colored Arabian horse with a distinctive white rose on its forehead.

The officer was a young colonel. His skin was smooth and unblemished. His eyes were ice blue and his cheek bones high. He sported a sculpted straw-colored mustache that matched the color of his flowing hair. His hands were smooth and feminine. Except for a cavernous space between his upper front teeth that produced word distortions and lisping sounds the colonel's teeth were well aligned. He wore a ceremonial uniform tailored more for parade than battle and a bejeweled saber that dangled from a brown leather belt tight around his waist.

The colonel was the scion of one the south's wealthiest families. Indulged and self-absorbed by any measure he financed his hedonistic pleasures with an unlimited family monetary allowance.

After years of lavish living in Europe the colonel returned home to what he believed was the winning months of the war, and to set in motion his ascendency to the presidency of the Confederacy.

At the war's conclusion the colonel envisioned his return to the south's exclusive smoking clubs and glittering balls where he would regale men and women with fanciful acts of bravery on the battlefield.

The colonel rationalized his elocution defect to the several languages he learned to speak while living in Europe. When agitated, the colonel's orders came across in a whistling lisp much to the amusement of the infantry soldiers, all of whom thoroughly detested him.

Considering army horses unsuitable, he brought with him from the family plantation, the Arabian. The colonel distained officers below the rank of general and held jaundiced views of officers he considered low-born.

Ignoring the colonel's prodding to move the Arabian stopped at Will's post. Irritated, the colonel yanked the Arabian around and spurred its sides drawing rivulets of blood that ran over older congealed punctures. He unsheathed and stabbed his saber into the air demanding the destruction of the enemy. He called the soldiers manning the defensive line dirt rats and lowlifes, which he spewed in a high-pitched whistling stream that came out, *dirt wats* and *wo wifes*. The soldiers exploded in volcanic laughter.

The colonel stared blankly into space his extended arm frozen in mid-air and for several minutes, he was catatonic like a stone monument of a dead military hero in a town square.

As quickly as the soldiers' laughter started it stopped, some of the men had pangs of conscience at the pathetic sight of the colonel shocked into suspended animation, while others a w a i t e d his next move.

"Colonel, y'all pointin' in the wrong direction! That's where our boys are!" With the unseen soldier's characterization, and the pitiable sight of the despised colonel, the soldiers burst into another chorus of laughter, aspersions and chanting.

The soldiers' derision thawed the colonel's catatonia. He fumbled then re-sheathed his saber to refrains of lusty laughter and ribald commentary.

Crimsoned in impotent rage the colonel dug his spurs into the Arabian. At the sight of the Arabian's suffering Will bit his lip. He recalled a happily anticipated event on the farm that turned to sadness when a foal was stillborn. The memory of Mary comforting the foal's mother, as she grieved flashed in his mind.

72

Witnessing the colonel's mistreatment o f t h e A r a b i a n , W i l l reached a flash point. He threw down his rifle and raced along the d u s t y road. T h e soldiers wondered what the colonel might do, as Will neared the Arabian.

"If he tries anything I'll blow the bastard's brains out," one soldier promised.

"Get in line," added another.

"Ah'm loaded and ready to let 'em have it," offered yet another.

Will took the Arabian's harness into his hands and stroked its neck and forehead as he and Mary had done for the foal's mother and the Arabian calmed. The soldiers erupted into whooping cheers. They pumped their rifles up and down and waved their garrison caps over their heads, shouting lustily, "Good Man! Good Man!"

The colonel glared at Will, his entire persona on fire. He vowed to even the score with the low-born farmer who had the temerity to challenge him.

"This isn't over!" the colonel screeched, his whistling lisp added a weird dimension to his threat.

"I'll see you, again! You can count on it! I'll see you, again!" The colonel screamed kicking Will to the ground, and then fleeing through a gauntlet of obscene-gesturing soldiers.

Chapter Sixteen

Bitter Mist

The Final Battle ~ Day Two

Virginia ~ Spring ~ 1865

An ammunition wagon lumbered along the rutted road between the woods and battle line. It stopped, like a street vendor open for business. Will rushed to the wagon and filled his cartridge case with rifle balls. Then he returned to his post to be alone with his thoughts as the reality of battle crept closer.

All of the soldiers seemed trapped in a time warp as if the world had spun down. In the eerie silence that permeated the defensive line Will glanced at a soldier looking his way. They winked at each other, and then both looked to the battered field ahead.

"Hey!" the soldier later called to Will, "Lookie at this," he held up a harmonica.

"You play that thing?"

"Y'all wait and see," the soldier said, tapping the harmonica several times on his leg. "Listen to this." He cupped the harmonica to his mouth and started playing.

"How's that?" asked the soldier.

"Real good," answered Will.

The soldier smiled and tapped his harmonica to clear its honeycomb cells, then raised the instrument to his mouth and breathed soft music into it. Its nostalgic sounds transported Will back to the excitement of the maturing peach orchard and how he badgered Father Vollmer with a fusillade of questions.

"When will the   peaches   come,   papa?" he remembered asking.

"What color will they be? When will the peaches come, papa?" he pestered.

"You must be patient, Will," Father Vollmer smiled, indulgently. "They will come when they are ready."

"They will come when they are ready. They will bring death, not sweetness," Will thought, his beating heart rising and falling as if synchronized to a clock that would tick the hour of his doom.

The soldier stopped playing his harmonica. An unsettling quiet consumed the men on the line. Then the soldier moved the harmonica briskly, across his mouth, blowing swift rhythmic melodies into the air.

Soldiers stepped onto the road, tapping their feet, taking partners and swinging one another around as if they were home at barn dances high on life, luxuriating in the soft embraces of their women, inebriated on apple jack and corn liquor.

The side trip to normalcy lasted only minutes. As quickly as it began, it ended. The soldier tapped his harmonica into the palm of his hand and brushed its silver plate.

75

"How was that?"

"Mighty good," Will answered.

"My last performance," the soldier said. He threw his harmonica over the fortification and watched it skip away. Will smiled, ironically. The soldier, with equal irony, smiled back. Then they resumed their silent watches of the sprawling field ahead, never speaking nor setting eyes on each other, again.

Orchestrated artillery sundered the fatalistic quiet that had descended on the soldiers. It blasted into positions along the defensive line. It blew fortification logs skyward, spinning in the air like helicopter blades before falling clumsily to the groaning earth below.

Will curled against the tree-laced fortification, his heart beating wildly. He closed his eyes and covered his ears to block out the sounds of concussive explosions that seemed to go on forever. Volleys struck from all directions, screaming into trenches, caving their sides into instant graves, burying soldiers whose last markings of their earthly existences were their bayonets protruding through the earth that covered them.

Artillery thundered relentlessly, splitting the heavens, spitting hot fire until cannon tubes hissed and cracked, and then, the exhausted guns fell silent.

A graveyard silence gripped the smoke-choked field. Will distrusted the artillery lull. He hugged the fortification like an obsessive lover. His head pounded and his heart raced. Sulfurous smog shielded the sun searing the eyes of the living, shrouding the soul-departed dead, obscuring the rutted road and the woods, beyond.

76

"Jeez!" What is that?" An unseen soldier's disembodied voice floated through the smoke.

"Don't look like anything from this world," another unseen voice exclaimed.

"It's the Good and Great Lawd! I tell ya' it's the Good and Great Lawd, come to take us home," screamed another soldier at the wraith-like figure wandering through the caustic clouds.

"No, it ain't! It's the devil his-self coming up from hell!" challenged another soldier, his widened eyes tracing the wraith coming closer to him the gray clouds of spent artillery fire smoking off his body, as if he were on fire.

"Ah'm getting' outa' here!" he cried out.

"No, ya' not, stay where ya' are!" ordered Sarge.

A skinny young soldier his arms hanging limp at his sides his palms upturned in a classic posture of disbelief came through the clearing smoke. He peered below his waist and exclaimed, "Good Lawd! Good Lawd!"

"Well, would ya' look at that. What's wrong with you?" queried another unseen soldier

"Ah' wet my-own self!"

"You did what?"

"Ah' said, I wet my-own self. Cain't ya' hear? Cain't ya' see?"

"Can't see nothin' in this soup. Where are you?"

"In Virginia, ah'm in Virginia."

"I know ya' in Virginia, dunce. Don't move we'll come for ya'," a voice snickered.

"Ah'm in the road, near my post."

"How do you know fer' sure ya' in the road? Can't see nothin' in this fog," another voice, unable to contain its amusement drifted through the vapor.

"Ah' know 'cause my foot is stuck in a wheel rut."

"So, y'all can't move," snickered another soldier.

The mist scattered in an unexpected breeze and the skinny young soldier and his soaked trousers came into sharper focus.

"Y'all funnin' with me, ain't ya? Cain't ya see, ah'm wetter than a hound dog on bath night."

"Well would ya' look what we have here," another voice guffawed. "Why – wouldn't ya' know it, we all discovered the Fountain of Youth."

"Now, what would his mama say?" the voice of another soldier chimed in.

"She be so embarrassed her little boy peed his-self and in public, no less," answered another.

"Shut up! All of you!" Sarge barked. "Get back to your post!" he ordered the young soldier.

"Did ya' hear them, Sarge? It ain't right."

"Get back to your post," Sarge ordered again, failing to contain his laughter.

"Right, Sarge, okay, Sarge, ah'm goin' back. It ain't right them funnin' me." The skinny young soldier extracted his foot from the wheel-rut.

"Ya' forgot something!"

Sarge tossed the soldier's boot to him.

The soldier retrieved his boot and crossed the road back to his post where teasing comrades buffeted him back and forth like a ping-pong ball.

"That's enough!" Sarge growled. "The rest of you numbskulls keep a sharp eye!" Sarge spit his order through clenched teeth, then he straightened his garrison cap and went back to his post, lit a cigar and awaited the inevitable.

"Sarge. Can we talk to ya'?" the Fountain of Youth soldier, now spokesman for a small group of young soldiers asked.

"You, again. Whadda ya' want?"

"Well," the Fountain of Youth shuffled his feet. "Here's the way it is. The blue boys stopped shellin'. Do ya' think, mebbe Mista Lincoln called off the rest of the war? It's been a long war."

Sarge blew a cloud of smoke into the air. He looked at the small group of soldiers in front of him, all skinny boys, none more than eighteen years.

"Nobody called off the war. The blue boys are gonna come at us, and they're gonna come soon."

"The boys want to know if all of us gonna make it, an' go home. Ya' know, go home, safe."

Sarge looked into the eyes of each of the soldiers, standing silently, rifles at their sides, all wanting to go home to farm the land, to roll in the hay with their girlfriends and live their allotted years in peace. Sarge didn't answer. He turned and walked away through wisps of bitter mist. The young soldiers went back to their posts.

Sarge foresaw their deaths.

Sweat and fear poured out of the soldiers like water trickling out of leaky faucets. Clothes stuck to bodies, brains flooded with fear, time crawled and thoughts came to the soldiers in jumbled dull flashes. They rammed cartridges down the throats of rifle muzzles and snapped bayonets onto barrel tips, the reports of cocking m u s k e t hammers clicked up and down the line.

Will thought about yesterday's rush of men and artillery into firing positions. He saw battered soldiers staring vacantly at the abused battleground.

How long would it take to run home to Mary and Will Jr.?" Will thought. "But, Mary and Will Jr. are gone." "How much longer will this war go on?" Will questioned.

"Maybe forever," he answered.

Will wondered if he would be alive when the sun went down.

Faces of dead comrades paraded before his open eyes. It seemed they had died an eternity ago, and the war had gone on just as long. He rested his face against his rifle and felt its coolness. He closed his eyes and saw Mary and his mother and father. He imagined Will Jr., the son he had never known and knew they would always be alive and treasured in his memory.

In dread stillness, eyes strained through puffs of floating mist at the field before them, waiting, all the time, waiting, hearing in their heads only the strange hum of the universe.

Chapter Seventeen

A Stranger in Two Worlds

Tongues of Fire

The Final Battle ~ The River Plain ~ Day Two

Virginia ~ Spring ~ 1865

Will's spirit left its earthly presence above the river plain and floated to wine-colored space that existed in a soundless vacuum. Two river branches joined together forming an arc around a green field. The river branches weren't wide, but its waters were deep. The trees overarching the riverbank stood deathly still.

On the river plain thousands of Confederate soldiers and hundreds of heavy and light artillery pieces massed together at one end of what seemed an endless stretch.

Will's spirit floated to the Union-end of the field where soldiers and horse-drawn artillery, like apparitions crossed the river taking up positions along its bank. Will's spirit levitated above the field witnessing in sorrow armies clashing below, spewing tongues of fire through a purplish haze.

"Ya' okay, Vollmer?" Sarge yelled.

"Yeah, Sarge. I'm all right."

"This is no time to be dreaming, Vollmer."

"Right, Sarge."

"The blue boys are comin'. Stay sharp, lad!"

"Okay, Sarge."

"Ya' sure?"

"Yeah, Sarge. I'm sure."

The field and the woods and the Union forces seemed unreal. Will tried to squint away the blurred currents produced in his brain. The war seemed far away, receding until everything connected to it devolved into insignificant specks.

The war was Will's unwanted reality.

He had become a stranger in two worlds.

Chapter Eighteen

Theater of His Mind

The Final Battle ~ Day Two

The River Plain ~ Spring ~1865

Future Time

From his post above the river plain Will heard the roar of artillery explosions and the crack of rifle fire, a strange juxtaposition to the eerie quiet on the upper ridge.

"I'm sweating," he thought, "I'm sweating in a cool spring morning." It seemed to Will all the men were sweating, slathered in sweat, sweating profusely, sweat, their baptism of fear. Despite his sojourn into timeless space Will's destiny remained imprisoned in an Aladdin cave of his mind.

"Stop dreaming, Vollmer!" Sarge rasped through cigar clenched teeth.

"I'm okay, Sarge."

Will turned to the sprawling field ahead and what he saw shocked his sensibilities. A curtain unfurled from high in the sky. It parted revealing a red tinted screen, onto which a beam of bright light with flickering images of the battlefield below the ridge shone on the screen.

In the theater of his mind Will was a powerless spectator unable to change the destinies of the men on the field. He viewed moving pictures of clashing soldiers and booms of artillery and crackling rifle fire and sweeping smoke enacted in the funereal silence of a cosmic vacuum where everybody and everything moved mournfully, lugubriously.

Will watched thousands of soldiers, like spring-wound dispirited automatons walk into rolling smoke, shredded by rifle and canister shot and slashing sabers, never again to respond to their names or to succumb to their desires, hearing only their last sorrowful screams superimposed on images of the architects of the war.

Then Will saw the future.

Soldiers firing their rifles from trenches across vast stretches of bomb-cratered land in France, and waves of soldiers storming beaches and parachuting from the sky in France and Italy, and soldiers raising a flag on a small sulfurous island in the Pacific, and freezing and frozen soldiers at a reservoir in Korea, and soldiers fighting in steaming jungles in Vietnam, and in boiling heat in Iraq and Afghanistan.

Will saw the battlefield he had fought on. It was a memorial where commemorative monuments dotted the landscape. He saw tourist information centers and wide-screen plasma televisions showing actors dressed as soldiers re-enacting battles. He saw modern cars and motorcycles with 2015 license plates from all over the United States. He saw tourists carrying s m a r t p h o n e s a n d digital cameras videotaping scenes and snapping photographs, wandering about, trying to imagine what had happened, before their time.

The battlefield was rich in artifacts.

Will saw young boys run breathlessly to their parents, clutching brass buttons and garrison cap bands and spent cartridges in their restless hands wanting to know to whom they belonged and were their owner's young men and did they have girlfriends and wives and sons and daughters.

Their parents answered.

"They were like us. I'm sure they had hopes and dreams. But now they are lost in memory. They have returned to the stars that gave them birth, and now, they belong to the ages."

Chapter Nineteen

Unseeing Eyes

The Final Battle ~ The Upper Ridge ~ Day Two

The Arabian's Revenge

Spring ~ 1865

Will's spirit returned to his post on the upper ridge, where he saw his incarnate self hollow of spirit, firing into tidal waves of Union soldiers that flooded the field, shooting and killing, mindlessly.

His spirit reached out to alert Will that soon he would face a sea of Union soldiers coming from the river plain below the ridge in overwhelming numbers to spring the trap that would cast him and his comrades into oblivion.

Will's spirit knew it had no physical presence on earth that it existed in infinity a consciousness born and nurtured in a timeless sphere. It looked long and sorrowfully at Will, the progenitor of his other consciousness frantically firing and reloading. Slowly, Will's spirit merged into his earthly presence becoming one with him, again.

Within hours Union soldiers broke through to the upper ridge and breached the salient where Will had been fighting overpowering its defenders, disabling everything in its way, driving inexorably forward to capture the heart of the Confederate army.

In the close fighting Will discerned the features of men who had been anonymous blurs. Despite the cauldron that was now his world he wondered if some supernatural force was protecting him. He questioned why he was untouched by the conflagration that consumed everything in its way. Then Will's animus consumed his splinter of rationality. He reloaded his rifle and aimed at a soldier coming through the rolling smoke.

The soldier walked nonchalantly through the burning mist. He was more apparition than flesh and blood. His blue uniform was ripped and burnt with countless bullet holes. The soldier carried no rifle. A peculiar smile creased his face. He looked long and spacey at Will through unseeing eyes.

For Will the battle had become a weird abstraction; his immunity to injury or death, a spectral soldier devoid of life. The roar of battle in Will's mind died. He could see, but he couldn't hear. He was trapped in a sound chamber, cut off from the chaos around him, severed from the hollering soldiers, the booms of artillery shells, the crackle of rifle fire, the cries of the wounded and the last screams of the dead.

The spectral soldier walked fluidly through the sweeping smoke as if floating on air. He came within touching distance of Will. They stared at each other. Will thought the soldier's eyes were two crystal pools that if he looked into them he would see his soul and learn the story of his life.

Rifle shot spattered through the soldier. A s he rounded the barricade Will lowered his rifle and pounded his head to bring hearing back into his brain.

He watched the soldier cross over the dusty road that separated the fortifications from the woods, unseen by attacking and retreating soldiers the soldier sailed across the field and disappeared into the woods.

The Confederate line dissolved in panic. Soldiers fled; some made it into the woods, others were not as lucky. Then Will's ears popped open. He heard the bugler's shrill retreat call. He remained stunned and disbelieving at his post, at the spectral soldier who had sought him out for some unfathomable reason.

The piercing notes of retreat reached the colonel, exploding derisively into his head, mocking him, divesting him of his arrogated entitlements, jeering the end of his quest for glory.

The colonel's world of fantastic imaginings consumed what was left of his sanity. In his twisted mind the retreating officers and soldiers conspired to deny him the grandeur he tasted sweet on his tongue. He drove the rebellious Arabian into flows of retreating soldiers, swinging his saber wildly, slashing everything and everyone in his path, screaming in a powerless rage.

Will tried to comprehend the incomprehensible; the soldier who was impervious to death, the soldier who sought him out for some unknown purpose. Will looked down the slope to the once green field now a blue tsunami coming to engulf him.

He backed away from his post still in a state of disbelief. When he turned to run into the woods his eyes widened at the shrieking colonel coming at him, digging his spurs into the Arabian.

"I said this wasn't over, farmer!" he screamed in a high-pitched whistling screech, pointing his saber at Will. Your payment is due," he shrieked, driving the uncooperative Arabian hard at Will.

"If I am to die," Will thought, "It's not going to be at the tip of the colonel's saber."

Will ran as fast as his legs could carry him.

The Arabian slowed the colonel's charge. Will escaped into the smoke-filled woods where he thought he had descended i n t o hell where amputated tree trunks leaned grotesquely against one another and burning fog drifted everywhere, soundless and creepy, onto a circle where the light of day had become a distant memory.

The colonel cantered deliberately toward Will, tormenting him, his lusting rage clinging like the perfume of an unforgivable sin. Will's legs caved and he fell backward. The colonel loomed over him, his bloodshot eyes popping in murderous rage. He raised his saber high above his head, to strike.

The Arabian's gyrations thwarted the colonel's death blow. His blade slammed sideways against Will's face knocking him to the ground. Will's head screamed in pain, blood cascaded down his face, sticky gore oozed into his mouth and down his throat jamming his windpipe.

The colonel raised his saber to strike again, to release the humiliation that had wormed its way into his mind and metastasized into the twisted canyons of his psyche. The Arabian reared up, on his hind legs, high into the burning fog, his forelegs flailing wildly, tumbling the colonel off his back, impaled on the tip of his bejeweled saber, his dreams of political conquest, fame and glory spilling with his life's blood into the tortured earth.

Will's world had become a miasma of unimagined pain; all about him was spinning, the Arabian spun like a horse on a race track, the trees in the woods spun like a green carousel, and the twinkling of musketry seemed like millions of cats-eyes blinking at him.

Will staggered to his feet, but he fell backward into the embrace of the colonel's lifeless body. He got up, but collapsed again landing face-to-face with the colonel, looking into his stunned dead eyes.

The Arabian knelt next to Will, snorting and prodding.

Will pulled himself up, onto the Arabian's back and they left the woods.

Chapter Twenty

Strange Encounter

Life's Ledger

Virginia ~ Spring ~ 1865

Will woke in an archway of trees that opened to a sparkling green meadow and a clear blue sky. All about him was dream-like. He touched the side of his face; its pain told him the colonel and the Arabian were not figments of his imagination. His head throbbed as if a frenzied drummer pounded mercilessly on it. He closed his eyes for relief, but the anesthesia of sleep eluded him. Against the base of a broad tree trunk the spectral Union soldier stared at Will, with vacant eyes.

"I know your thoughts," Will hollered.

"I have come to beg your forgiveness."

"Who are you? I don't know what you mean."

"You have a letter in your pocket."

Will's hand shot to his pocket.

"What do you know of the letter in my pocket?"

"We are all one." the soldier's thought formed in Will's mind.

"Look at me! Tell me what you see."

"A lifeless soldier in a blue uniform."

"What else do you see?"

"I don't know what you mean."

"The insignias on my uniform; what do you see?"

"A glitter on your garrison cap."

"Can you read the insignia?"

"No."

"Try again."

Will squeezed his lids tight provoking a surge of pain. Then the insignia on the soldier's cap came into focus and what he saw paralyzed his thoughts and arrested his pain. Will couldn't answer, words wouldn't come.

"It says New Jersey – 13," the soldier said.

Will would never forget Mother Vollmer's words; they were forever seared in his memory. The image of that dark night flashed into his mind, father at the well, the frightened Union soldier from New Jersey, it all came back in wrenching detail. Will looked at the lifeless soldier sprawled against a tree trunk in front of him.

"You and this war destroyed my life," Will shouted, "My life is no longer worth living."

"It was my bullet that claimed your father's life. I am forever scarred," the telepathy of the soldier's thought, tinged in sorrow echoed in Will's mind.

93

"I buried your Mary and her baby, your infant son, and your mother and father in an early morning sunrise in the shade of the peach orchard next to baby girl's grave. I was the last mortal on earth to see and touch them."

"What do you want with me? Haven't you done enough?"

"We have an eternal bond," the soldier communicated, "I have come to beg your forgiveness."

"You have come for my forgiveness," Will answered, disbelieving the soldier's request.

"Yes, I have come for your forgiveness."

"Why do you need my forgiveness?"

"I was frightened then, as I am frightened now, frightened that you will not agree to my petition

"Your request is for a selfish purpose?" Will quizzed.

"All requests for forgiveness are selfish; the true test is sincerity, with your forgiveness I can access powers for good that I can deliver on earth, powers beyond human imagination. Without your forgiveness I am condemned to wander, unredeemed, for all eternity."

Will labored over the inspirations that came to him from the lifeless soldier. He understood fear; it had contaminated his soul, fear was his constant companion and he wanted to evict it from his life.

"I have no powers."

"But you do," the soldier countered, telepathically. "You have one of the greatest powers of all, the power to forgive."

"How does one forgive his father's killer? Mother forgave the soldier," Will reflected, "Who am I not to forgive him? Will the spirits of those I killed forgive me? I hope soldiers unknown to me will be generous of heart for their deaths are not my sins. They are the sins of those who seek self-glorification, those who to themselves would build monuments."

The throbbing pain in Will's head returned. He closed his eyes for a long time and stopped thinking. Silent space existed between him and the soldier across from him waiting for Will's reply, hoping for his absolution.

"You have my forgiveness," Will said, opening his eyes. "All of us need forgiveness. I struggle to recall the joys of my life. Their memories are dim and I cannot touch them. I am trapped in a forest of despair; eyes are on me all the time, haunting me. I cannot be where I long to be. I have no home. All roads lead nowhere."

"The mind is fickle," counseled the soldier. "Home is in the true heart. You are locked in time. The difference between your past and present and the days to come is nothing more than an annoying illusion."

"What do you mean?"

"We are all immortal; the soldiers we killed are immortal, all of the dead on the battlefields from the beginning of time are immortal. Like me, they live forever in universes beyond the hand of time."

"I want to see Mary, again. Can you understand how difficult it is to miss someone you love and desire their return, which will never come? I want to touch her. I want to hold her. I want to hold my infant son," Will said, his answer a mixture of lament and demand.

"We are all born of a single universal soul. We carry within us fragments of each other. In your journey Mary will come to you as will those you love so well with messages that will dispel your doubts."

"Do you have regrets?" Will asked.

"Yes, I have regrets."

"Were they of your own making?"

"I wish I could get back some of the things I did. I wish I could get back some of the things I said. I never knowingly or maliciously did anyone harm."

"Then what do you regret?"

"I wish I could have lived out my missed years."

"Your missed years?"

"My life ended at eighteen. I wonder what I would have been had I lived to nineteen or to thirty."

"You must know from where you are now."

"Our bodies are corruptible, but our minds are pure energy, we never die. Your forgiveness frees me to visit universes beyond the short reach of time. I can come to know and live out those missed years."

"Why don't you?"

"I never knew what you and Mary experienced. The bliss of human love and the pangs of sorrow that is life's ledger," the soldier replied.

"I have felt love, but now my love is lost."

"Love never dies."

"But not as it once was," Will contested.

"It will be that way again."

"My life is a tortured journey," Will said, a note of defeat in his voice.

"You may not see it now. You will make a difference.

"I'm just a farm boy. What difference can I make?"

"The greatest differences made on earth are small victories woven into tapestries of great accomplishments. Your forgiveness has lifted a great weight from me. It has unchained me to learn the mysteries of countless universes. You are my brother; we share an eternal bond, we are a single coin with distinctive sides."

Will drifted into a deep sleep. When he woke he poured water from his canteen over his face. He felt a gentle breeze on his face. The maelstrom of his confusion had subsided, but hadn't resolved. Will sensed a long and lonely journey ahead.

"Maybe, sometime, somewhere, I will make a difference," he thought.

The soldier was gone. Will pushed himself up on his rifle, still woozy from the colonel's blow to his head. He fired his last cartridge into the air and let the rifle slip from his hands to be discovered sometime in the unknowable future, a rusted artifact of an unknown soldier who fought in a great war.

Will's war ended, but his lonely life had begun. In the meadowland he wove his way through pockets of vanquished soldiers. A strange silence hung in the air. He came to the edge of the field and looked back to the arboreal passageway, which like the spectral soldier had disappeared from earthly reality. He felt a tug on his trousers and looked down to where a toothless soldier, his steel-gray eyes bouncing crazily in their sockets, sat lotus-like, on the ground.

"I'm going home," he yammered, giddily. "Y'all going home, too?" he cackled, monotonously.

Will wondered if the crazy soldier was a portent of his life.

He pulled away and left the field.

Chapter Twenty One

My Life is Empty Without You

Desire and Guilt

Virginia ~ Spring ~ 1865

Will looked back at the field of broken men. The crazed soldier's cackling still rang inside his head. Will walked a long way, for a long time, before the soldier's echo faded from his mind. He felt his spirit had been sucked out of him and his soul consigned to a dark recess with no chance of resurrection. In the day's gathering darkness Will found a place on the edge of the road. He lay down and drifted into a troubled sleep.

When he woke, Will walked the sun-soaked highway. "I'm alive," he thought, "But, am I?" he questioned, "I'm lost. I'm dead, inside."

Will believed he was stuck in a nightmare. He hoped to awaken and find nothing had changed. He envisioned Father Vollmer in the peach orchard and Mother Vollmer tending her flower garden.

"Get up, sleepyhead! Get out of bed!" Will heard Mary's voice resonate in his mind.

"I don't know where I am going," Will's lurking tragedies re-emerged

Below a bend in the sweltering highway Will heard rushing water and followed its sound to a rocky stream that emptied into a hidden river.

At the river's edge Will stripped off his clothes and pounded them on glistening rocks and hung them to dry on hanging willow branches. He secured Mother Vollmer's letter under his garrison cap with a rock.

Then he waded into the river and immersed himself.

"It's hot and the water is cold," he thought.

Will sank under its surface and came up several times before floating on his back.

"Birth must be this way; floating, protected. Then with the first breath comes life's pain."

Will thought about his infant son.

He welcomed the warm sun on his face and the floating sensation and the forgetfulness both brought him.

However, neither was destined to last.

A young woman swept her hands and arms in slow arcs beneath the hidden river's surface. She propelled herself to Will. Her long hair floated on the water's surface like an open fan and her eyes reflected the sun's glint. She circled Will like a huntress and smiled enigmatically. She splashed water on Will's face, laughing softly as she completed her encirclement. The woman circled, again, running her hands soothingly across Will's shoulders, across his back and chest and over his wounded face as Will's passion rose in the heat of the day's radiant sun.

The woman sank below the water's surface, and then she emerged, her face gleamed in the sunshine.

Will closed his eyes and felt the water rippling against his body as the woman continued her encirclement. He felt her soft breath on his face and her warm embrace drawing his nakedness against her's.

"Mary," Will whispered.

The woman kissed the wound on Will's face.

"I am Mary," she pressed her lips to Will's. "I am Mary," she kissed Will's mouth.

The woman's kiss transported Will to the sunny spring day when Mary kissed him, and their kisses transported them into a world of ethereal bliss and revelation.

"You have come back to me, Mary," Will said. "I want to be with you."

"I am here," the woman extended her hand to Will.

"Come with me."

Will was caught in a web of desire and guilt.

The woman whispered, comfortingly, "I am Mary. Come with me."

"You are not Mary!" Will shouted.

They looked into each other's eyes, both naked in their desires, and again, the woman held out her hand and beckoned to Will.

"Come with me."

Will stared at the woman standing in the water before him. He recalled his love and desire for Mary.

"You've come back to me, Mary."

"I have come for you," the woman said, holding out her hand.

Then an unseen force pushed Will into the rocky stream, beyond the line separating the mortal and immortal worlds.

Will reached for the woman, but mortality's grip was irresistible and the woman disappeared.

"I want to be with you, Mary," Will cried out, "my life is empty without you."

Chapter Twenty Two

Tangled Web on a Forgotten Highway

A Cosmic Orphan

Virginia ~ Spring ~ 1865

Will sat in the stream's rushing water gazing at the lusterless river. He didn't know how long he was there or how far he walked since leaving the Virginia battlefield. In the fading day Will dressed and climbed to the highway.

As darkness closed in the nocturnal sounds of the woods came to life. Small animals crackled on fallen leaves and deer brushed through vegetation in search of water.

Will sat against a wide-base tree trunk. He built a fire of dry leaves and twigs and curled next to it to sleep and to breathe in the narcotic of forgetfulness.

In the night, jagged streaks of light flashed. The heavens roared like a prowling pride of a thousand lions, harbingers of rain to come. Wind whistled through the woods where Will lay lost in fitful sleep. Lightning split the sky in long white arcs and crooked spears. Thunder boomed, boisterous and relentless, shaking the night. Wind whipped through the woods scooping and tossing underbrush, scattering fallen leaves, creating dark illusions of dancing trees, at one moment shadowy black and then ghostly white against the flashing sky.

103

The unsettled night thundered in Will's mind eliciting memories of artillery spitting fire and belching its caustic breath. He saw Mary and their son, and Mother and Father Vollmer waving goodbye and then disappearing into a white cloud. He tightened his fetal position until his knees and chin almost touched. He whimpered at each spasm of light and shuddered at each boom of thunder.

Will didn't wake and cleansing rains never came from the sterile night.

Like a cranky child the woods woke. The sun sparkled through leafy tree patches. The trilling of birds came first to Will as distant music of a new day, and then as wake-up calls. He opened his eyes to a squirrel standing on its hind legs, still as a statue. They eyed each other; Will, curiously, the squirrel, suspiciously. At the sight of the inquisitive squirrel Will's lips creased into a rare smile. He tossed a twig and the squirrel ran away.

Will's thoughts came in jumbled spurts. The strips of bark he ate failed to quell his hunger, he thirsted, but his canteen was empty.

"If I don't get out of here, I will die, undiscovered and unknown," he thought.

Will started out of the woods. He tripped over brambles. Buzzing insects tormented him. When he faltered he pulled himself up on hanging vines. When he tired he rested against ageless tree trunks. The woods had become Will's nemesis and his ally.

Will climbed to the highway.

The early morning light cast a golden patina on the highway that swung in a wide northeasterly arc, before rising gradually, and then sloping gently to where the woods met a trackless *terra cota*-colored surface.

The dull pain of the colonel's saber persisted; it blurred Will's vision and caused sporadic dizziness. He looked around, and behind him, for signs of life. Will saw only regiments of young men slow-walking through shimmering bluish mists their faces drained of being and he saw the saber-swinging colonel coming at him, blood-lust in his eyes. Will walked as fast as his weakened body permitted, trying to get away from the ghosts chasing him, trying to unlock his incarcerated mind, but finding no exit.

Will tried to remember who he had been and he wondered what he had become. But for screeching insects hot in the woods and chirping birds in treetops the highway seemed a cosmic orphan forgotten by time.

He picked up a branch on the highway and swung it side-to-side as he had when a boy in Georgia. He remembered running through meadows striking at wildflowers, feeling the planet vibrating beneath his feet and radiant heat on his face certain he was one with the earth and the sky, confident of his immortality.

Will's reminiscence of his youth transported him into a dimension of forgetfulness. In the shade of high-crowned trees where the woods leveled to the highway, Will came to a rock ledge and stopped to rest.

As dusk came to the highway all about it deepened; the green of the woods turned greener, the song of birds sharper in the comfort of their nests as the day turned to darkness.

Will scratched the tip of his branch through the clay. He drew a tangled web of swirls and serpentine lines. When finished, he thought he had drawn a picture of his mystified existence. Will swept his foot through the clay erasing the irrational jumble leaving the earth smooth and unblemished.

Then his mind went blank.

When he returned to awareness, Will etched, again. He created his farmhouse, the peach orchard, the willow tree and the silvery stream. He remembered the joys and pleasures, the laughter and the memories and above all, his forever moments with Mary.

Cold and exhausted and still clutching his branch Will lost his struggle to stay awake.

"Are you all right?"

Will flinched like an irritated child, prodded from sleep. Then he calmed to the feel of a warm hand on his cold face.

"Mary!" Will murmured. "Mary," he repeated, returning to awareness.

He heard the voice, again, as if coming from a distant place.

"Are you all right?"

Will's eyes opened to a wagon with glowing lanterns on either side. It was burdened with small pieces of furniture and a provisions chest. Pots and pans dangling from its side, clinked rhythmically in occasional breezes.

106

A small boy with a haunted expression stared at Will. He sat next to an old mustached man who wore a white brimmed hat pulled tight on his head. The old man's face showed deep streams of a difficult life, and yet, it had an open and generous quality. A tethered team of gray horses waited, patient and incurious, their warm breathing vaporized into the cold night, their long manes limp on their broad shoulders.

A woman removed her hand from Will's face, and then she spoke to her father.

"Pa, he is weak and cold, he needs food and rest," she exclaimed.

The woman was tall and slender, more resilient than delicate. She wore a loose-fitting blue dress with small rose-colored floral designs. Her auburn hair was full. Untamed curls danced against her forehead in the night's easy breezes. Her eyes were warm and her smile bright and reassuring.

The woman looked at Will's drawing in the clay.

"Is this your home?" she asked.

"It was my home."

"Girl!" the old man bellowed from the wagon.

"You tell that boy, a' sittin' there on that rock to come with us. He can't stay out here. He'll freeze his-self ta' death if he stays out here. Now, you tell him that!" And then the old man busied himself slicing pieces of bread off a large loaf and cuts off a smoked sausage.

"Pa wants you to come with us," the woman said, "It's too cold out here, you are hungry and tired," She extended her hand, her eyes imploring Will to accept her invitation.

Will looked at the old man and the small boy, and then back to the woman. He dropped the branch and took her hand. When they touched an electrical current went through them.

"Well, is he a-comin'? We got a ways to go till campin' tonight," the old man bellowed, irascibly, handing the amputated pieces of bread and sausage to the small boy.

"You all wore out and skinny as a scarecrow," the old man appraised Will's condition. "Boy's got some food fer' ya' an' he'll keep ya' company. Ah' made some room at the back of the wagon," the old man said. "The boy don't talk, but he's a good little boy, an' faithful as a puppy."

"Girl!" the old man barked, "Get blankets fer' these boys, an' one fer' yerself. It's getting' mighty cold, now. An' girl, you ride up front with me. Wrap yerself warm, too. Ya' hear me, girl, an' none of yer' usual back talk from ya'."

"Yes, Pa," the woman agreed. "You best wrap yourself warm, too, Pa," s h e i s s u e d a velvet order, with a mirthful chuckle.

"Ya' always know how to rile yer' ole' pa up, don't ya', girl? Ah' don't need no blanket; my skin is like leather. Chill can't get through to me. Git yourself up there girl," the old man pointed to the driver's bench. "I'm gonna check the team and the wagon, an' we'll git on our way.

The old man was a dark silhouette in the moonlight at the back of the wagon going about his routine check. The small boy snuggled under Will's arm, warm against his body.

"Keep those blankets tight roun' both of ya'. We'll be out till we come to a spur to camp," the old man said, solemnly.

"Thank you, sir," Will said.

"What fer'?" the old man answered.

"I couldn't have made it through the night out here."

"Ah!" he waved his hand, dismissively, "Don't think about it. Get some sleep, like the boy, he's a smart little critter, sleeping away an' leavin' it to us to find our way outa' here," the old man looked at the sleeping boy, affectionately. "He don't or he won't speak. I don't know which, but he's a good boy." Will looked at the small boy, now sleeping fitfully, oblivious to the night.

"Where are we?" Will asked.

"Comin' to the Maryland border," the old man pointed ahead. "We should get there with the noonday sun."

"The Maryland border."

"The Maryland border is where we're a' headed. "Peers' ya' walked clear through Virginey," the old man patted Will's knee. "Small wonder yer' so tired and hungry. Now get yerself some sleep. I'm gonna check the wagon and the team, and we'll be gettin' along.

"Goodnight, sir."

"We'll see bout' that," he laughed.

Whenever he stopped the old man inspected the wagon. He watered the horses and patted their broad shoulders to show his appreciation for their long years of faithful service.

The horses were rare twin foals. No one in the County had ever heard of twin foals. The twins were the old man's loyal friends. He returned their fealty with concern and affection. In harness the twins' rhythmic clip-clop came as music to his ears.

The old man climbed on the driver's bench and took the reins in his hands. He shot a sly look to his daughter, at his side.

"Keep that blanket about yer' throat or you'll come down with the chills."

"I'll look like a papoose if I pull the blanket any higher, Pa."

"All this back talk, never doin' what yer' pa sez."

The woman pulled the blanket about her throat. "There, are you satisfied, now?" she smiled at her father, and smiled secretly to herself.

"Ar-ff'," the old man shrugged his shoulders and let the reins fall gently on the backs of the twins. The wagon jolted forward. Will felt the small boy's soft breathing and thought of his lost infant son. A gust of wind rolled along the highway dusting over Will's etchings in the clay leaving his home buried forever in the yesterdays of his life.

The wagon lumbered away. The twins ambled dutifully their steps in unison. The old man looked at his sleeping daughter, her head lolling to the wagon's motion, a sentimental smile on his face. He looked back at Will and the small boy. With each movement his arthritic neck snapped like an elastic band. In a nostalgic voice the old man spoke to the twins.

"Darnedest thing ~ this thing called life," the old man raised and let fall the reins to get the attention of the twins. "When we was young and full of vinegar and our juices were hot we took care of the younguns' and now we are old an' our limbs and bones creak like rusty gates an' we have aches and pains every day, all the time, an' ya' know what, we still takin' care of the yunguns'. Now, understan' I'm glad to do it."

Reflectively, the old man paused. His warm breath vaporized into the chilled night. He looked again at his sleeping daughter her body swaying to the gentle movement of the wagon.

The old man raised and lowered the reins on the backs of the twins.

"It was to be a great day, warm and sunny it was the whole world at my fingertips. Didn't ask for much; never asked for much, just a quiet life. Then it all come a tumbling' down; it all broke apart. My beautiful bride of only one year," his voice cracked, "Only one year! We had only one year!" he paused.

"She looked at the baby in her arms an' she smiled, and then she looked at me, an' she smiled, an' then just like that," he snapped his thumb and middle finger, "just like that, she closed her eyes. I thought she was tired from givin' birth and needed rest, but she closed her eyes for all time, never opening them to see her baby, to see me, again. I went outside to the porch an' that's where I was, wonderin' why the good Lord picked on us in such a cruel way. Then I heard her cryin', an' her cryin' brought me back, an' I went into the house. I picked up our baby girl, beautiful like her mama." The old man looked again at his daughter, peacefully asleep. "An' our baby girl, well she stopped her crying an' she gives me a big smile, no teeth, ya' understand, but the biggest most beautiful smile I ever saw, an' then she went to sleep in my arms."

"Smart little thing growin' up. We'd ride her to the schoolhouse, an' then pick 'er up when school let out," he reminded the twins who sauntered tranquilly along the dark highway.

"The school marm said she was perky an' as bright as a sunny day. Good at everythin', readin', writin', figurin'. She gobbled up her readers faster than her breakfast an' we'd go to the schoolhouse an' ask for more readers. The school marm was a handsome woman an' she really liked my little girl. Everybody said she wanted to marry up with me an' be mama to my little girl."

"Ya' listenin'?" the old man demanded of the twins.

Both nodded their heads, up and down.

"My heart is occupied. There is only one woman in it, an' she is gone from life, but not from my heart, where she always lives," he touched his chest.

"Yup. She lives in my heart. No vacancy sign is posted. Yes, sir! No Vacancy!"

The old man's lids came down and he fell asleep.

The wagon continued through the inky night, up gentle inclines, down subtle slopes and along rimming curves.

Suddenly, the twins stopped.

Chapter Twenty Three

I'll Worry for You

Strange Feelings

Virginia/Maryland Border

Spring ~ 1865

The wagon idled in the moonlight, its shadow long on the road. Sensing it had stopped, the old man woke up.

While Will, his daughter and the small boy slept, the old man examined the circumference around the wagon, and the highway's nearby peripheries. In the lantern's yellow light he saw a wheel-rutted path bending easily into the woods.

"Pa! What's wrong?" the old man's daughter woke, her voice suffused with sleep.

"Twins come to a stop at a cutoff," he raised his lantern showing the crossroad. "Likely in there," he pointed, "is a place to camp. I'll go see. You stay put, girl."

"I'll come, Pa!" the woman began climbing down from the wagon.

"No! You won't. That's my word an' you honor it. None of your usual back talk, you hear me?" the old man commanded.

"Alright, Pa," the woman acquiesced. With a sense of unease she watched him cross the road to the intersection into the woods.

"I'll go with you," Will said, coming from the side of the wagon.

"Glad for the company. I'm not a young man, anymore. Good to have someone to share the jitters."

"I'll get the boy!" the woman said, rounding the wagon to its back, where the small boy slept. The old man and Will walked side-by-side, trailing the lantern's glow, their senses keen to the life of the dark woods into which the light of an apathetic moon failed to penetrate. Will looked back to the wagon, its lantern light soft on the woman cradling the small boy in her arms.

Proudly, the old man exclaimed, "She'll be all right, strong and smart, she is."

Both men ignored the nighttime symphony of the woods, the screeching of small animals and its occasional mournful breezes. A black blur shot across their path, it cut noisily through the woods and soon faded away. Will and the old man exchanged nervous glances, and then they continued into the woods the lantern light illuminating their way.

Fearful of the night and threatened by demons that ransacked his memory the small boy woke up, crying.

Will looked at the old man.

"Should we go back?"

"The girl knows what to do, it happens most nights, the wakin' and the cryin'. The boy saw the horrors. I tell ya', the boy saw the horrors. He don't talk at all, but he wakes and cries every night. Don't worry, son, the girl knows what to do. Let's go, we have work to do."

The old man swung the glowing lantern back and forth, shining light on wheel ruts that revealed an open space at its north rim.

"Boy's sleepin', now, he's quieted down," the old man said.

"Guess he's all right."

"Girl knows what to do."

Across the road Will and the old man came to a pungent smelling fire pit.

"Man-made camp," the old man observed.

"Looks like it," Will agreed.

The old man swung his lantern in a wide arc to a wheel-rutted crescent-shaped line where the woods met the camp. "This is where the wagons drove in an' outa' the camp," he traced the arc with his free hand. "I can tell by the wheel tracks a comin' and a goin', there an' there," he said. "We'll set up and camp here fer' the night."

"If I didn't know better I'd say we at the Maryland border," the old man raised his lantern to the road, ahead.

"This is a west road," he pointed. "We are at the Maryland border. The twins pulled us a long way."

"Are you goin' west?" Will asked.

"Goin' west," the old man said, "a fresh start for the girl and the boy."

"What about you?" Will asked. "A fresh start for you, too?"

"Me!" the old man exclaimed, shaking his head, left to right. "Too late for me, too old to start new, too fixed in my ways. What you'll find out, son, is what all of us discover, some sooner than others that in the end we all become we were meant to be. Some are lucky and they find out early in life, that is, if life don't git in their way. Others come to know themselves after a long journey. Yes, sir! All of what I am is to git the girl and the boy a fresh start. Yes sir, that's who I am."

"What about you, son?"

"I don't know. I don't know," Will repeated.

"Well, let's bring the wagon here." The old man paused and laughed. "Darn smart twins. They know'd where I wanted to stop, an' they stopped, an' I was a sleepin'," he said, shaking his head, laughing softly.

"I'll take the twins in by the yoke," the old man said. "Son, you hold the reins steady so the twins know to take my lead."

"Alright," Will answered.

Will climbed aboard the wagon and he sat next to the woman and the boy, now fitfully asleep in her arms. They smiled at each other, and then they looked away.

The woman pressed the boy against her bosom. She stroked his face and whispered comforting shushes when he flinched in his sleep.

Weeks before stopping for Will, the old man found the boy wandering and disoriented, traumatized in the chaotic aftermath of a great battle. In many ways, Will's losses mirrored those of the old man.

He glanced at the woman and sensed her womanly presence. He recalled the warmth of her hand on his face. In the soft light, he thought her more beautiful than when first he opened his eyes to her touch. In his vision, the old man's daughter was Mary holding their slumbering son as they traveled home through a star-filled night. And as quickly as the vision came to Will, it dissolved.

"Are you cold?" Will asked.

"A little."

"I'll get another blanket."

"We'll be camping soon, I'll be all right till then," the woman pulled the boy closer to her.

"There's a fire pit where we're going."

The woman smiled at Will.

"A warm fire will feel good," she said.

"Don't have all night out here! If we don't git a movin' daylight will be on us. Now, tense those reins, and let's be on our way," the old man barked.

Will and the woman looked at each other suppressing spontaneous snickers at the old man's impatience and irascible annoyance.

Will tensed the twins' reins and the wagon swept into the darkness. Gullies crammed with soggy leaves lined both sides of a narrow path. The woods throbbed with scratching crickets. The wagon's wheels groaned as the twins pulled it along the tenuous edges of the narrow path. Earth crumbled beneath the wagon's weight. The crickets in the woods chirped louder.

The twins stopped. In the lantern's light the old man saw earth on the driver's side of the wagon sliding into the gully.

"Wagon's gonna tip over if'n we don't get all four wheels on solid ground," the old man observed. "Got a hair of space over there," he pointed to the passenger side of the wagon. "If'n we pull her that away," he slanted the lantern, "an' she comes up, then all four wheels will be on solid ground. Gotta get the back wheel off the edge, or sure as the sun come up tomorra' she's gonna tip over."

"Might help if I push from the side," Will proposed.

"If'n she goes over, son, ya' be buried under everything."

The woman looked at Will, concern flooded her face. She pressed the small boy to her and felt the commingling of their beating hearts. Will returned her worried look with a slight smile.

"I don't think the wagon will come up without a push from the side," he said.

"Alright!" the old man shook his head in agreement.

"Let's git' her on the path. Girl!" he called out, "You and the boy come down here."

The woman eased herself to the edge of the driver's bench. Will helped her off the wagon. In the instant they touched they knew that somewhere beyond time they had been lovers. Will and the woman held each other's hand, both refusing to let go.

"We'll set out when they are ready," the old man whispered to the twins, stroking their manes, uncharacteristically patient.

Reluctantly, Will and the woman let go of each other.

Will went to the other side of the wagon.

"I'll worry for you!" she shouted.

The sound of the woman's voice stopped Will. He looked back at her silhouetted in the moonlight holding the small boy. Without responding he walked past the old man, "I'll push, you pull," he said.

The slippery leaves in the gully defeated Will's efforts. The wagon remained unmovable, tilting at a dangerous angle.

"I have to try, again," Will thought, "if I don't, we'll be marooned here like a ship wreck on some unknown island."

"Let's give it a try!" he called out.

120

The old man brought the twins to him. The earth beneath the turning wheels began crumbling, and the wagon shifted sideways knocking Will to the ground.

The old man tightened his grip on the yoke. The twins stopped. The boy stirred. The woman held him tighter. The crickets in the woods quieted, and the night became strangely silent.

"What's happenin' son?"

"Pa! What's happening?"

"I'll go see," the old man said.

"Hold still!" he admonished the twins.

"Let's try, again," Will shouted.

"Alright, son," the old man replied.

"Alright," Will copied the old man's agreement.

"Pa!"

"We're gonna try, again."

"You tell me when, son!"

"Bring the twins to you. I'll push against the wagon."

The wagon remained tilted, and the earth beneath its wheels continued sliding into the gully. Then it began righting itself. Will looked up and saw it moving autonomously, defying the pull of gravity.

"I'll try, again!" Will yelled.

The old man tugged the twins' yoke and they came to him, but the wagon remained stuck.

Then Will felt a powerful force had joined his efforts. The old man held the twins' pace as the wagon's wheels rotated. Will pushed against its side and the wagon turned away from the gully's slope.

In the distance, the boy cried and the woman whispered comforting assurances to him. The wagon rolled on the narrow road, and the crickets in the woods resumed their nocturnal symphony.

Will watched the wagon roll past the woman, and the boy she held in her arms. Her words, "I'll worry for you," echoed in his mind. The woman and the boy consumed Will's thoughts. He quickened his steps and grew nearer to her. She became unsettled by her strange feelings.

The woman handed Will the sleeping boy, he kissed his forehead, the boy's trembling ceased, and he breathed quietly, untroubled.

Will embraced the woman; he felt her hand on his heart and her tears on his face.

"I worry for you throughout eternity," she whispered.

Chapter Twenty Four

Sleep Beside Me Tonight

Kaleidoscope of Her Life

Virginia/Maryland Border

Spring ~ 1865

At the campsite the old man unharnessed and covered the twins in thick blankets. The woman covered the boy and placed him next to the fire pit; she stroked his hair and kissed his pale cheeks.

"I knew we would be together, again," she said, softly.

Will piled split logs, dry brush and twigs into the fire pit, struck a spark, fire flared, and then it dropped. Will struck another spark and fire scurried along the split logs and erupted in flames their orange light glimmering on the crown of the fire pit.

The old man squatted in the warmth of the pit's flames. He rubbed his hands and pressed them to his face.

"Feels good," he said, rising with difficulty.

"Gonna get some sleep. Sun gonna' be up soon," he started to the wagon, and then he stopped, and said to Will.

"That was mighty brave, son, pushin' and rightin' the wagon, gettin' it on level ground. Ah' couldn't have done it without you."

"Thank you, sir."

"An' them twins. Ain't they the wonders? They know'd where to stop even though I was a sleepin'," he said as if confessing his sin.

"Don't be so hard on yourself, pa!" his daughter said.

"Well! I'm turnin' in. Son, you welcome to come with us." The woman looked at her hands smoothing her dress to demonstrate her disinterest in Will's response to her father's offer.

"Don't rightly know where we'll end up," the old man continued, "It will be away from the shootin' and killin'," his face dark beneath the brim of his white hat, fire light dancing in his tired eyes.

"Thank you for your offer."

"Well, think on it. I'm gonna get some sleep, ancient sun always keeps its time."

The old man walked back to the wagon.

Will sat next to the flickering fire. He buried his head in his hands, his mind a blank. He smiled at the woman at his side. She looked, first to the sleeping boy, and then at her hands, still smoothing her dress.

The woman took a deep breath before she spoke.

"Is Mary your wife?" she asked, remembering Will's waking response to her hours before on the highway.

Will didn't answer.

"I shouldn't have asked," the woman said, after an uncomfortable silence.

"Sorry if I made you uneasy," Will apologized.

"Mary and I planned to marry in the first spring after I returned from the war," he said, wistfully. "Mary loved the peach orchard on the farm. She was excited to be married when the flowers were blooming."

"The women looked away, tears welling in her eyes.

Will retreated into silence.

"If you don't want to talk anymore, I'll understand."

"We grew up together. Mary came to us when she was five years old, on New Year day. Mother wanted to keep Mary and father wanted to obey the laws about abandoned children. It was the only time they had a tense conflict, but it didn't last long. Nobody came for Mary. We were raised as brother and sister. Mary knew how to wind me up. We were always fighting. In our hearts we knew we meant more to each other than brother and sister."

The woman no longer heard the throbbing sounds of the woods, or the old man's snoring, or the easy breathing of the boy at her side.

She heard only Will.

125

"Mary was beautiful; life shined in her eyes. Ma would always be putting pink ribbons in her hair, like the one in your hair."

Will paused.

"We had a son," Will said in a breaking voice. "Days after our boy was born, he and Mary came down with the fever, and so did ma. Pa went to the well, and while there, a Union soldier shot him. Before the day had ended they were all gone."

Will lowered his head.

The woman placed her hand on Will's shoulder.

"You loved Mary," she said.

In a soft voice, Will said yes.

"You must know Mary's love for you is timeless. It distresses me to see you pained," the woman couldn't finish her thought.

"On the day I was born, my mother died," the woman said. "I wish she was with me now. When school let out I saw how my playmates' mamas picked them up and swung them around. I wished mama could be with me, to hug me and swing me around."

"I'm sorry you never knew your mother," Will said. "It must have been difficult for you."

"Townsfolk said it was a shame; a girl with no mother, but they were wrong, I know mama is a part of me.

I thought if I wished long enough and closed my eyes real tight, she would come to me, but she was some place where I couldn't reach her. Before I'd go to sleep she'd come to me. I'd feel her presence. In the morning I'd describe what she was wearing and how she combed her hair to pa, and he'd say, "How'd you know those things about your mama?" she paused in her remembrance.

"Ma's baby girl died the day she was born," Will said. "She suffered for a long time, and then out of nowhere, Mary showed up. Ma said she came to us from beyond the stars."

"Pa said the same thing about mama. He said she came to him from a special place. It was only mama he ever wanted in his life. He said no one could ever take her place, and then he'd say, my heart is occupied, no vacancy."

"Your pa raised you by himself?"

"He did, school plays, tea parties, the things young girls do. Pa is a special man," she paused, and smiling at her father's snoring, added, "I love him, dearly."

"We should get some sleep. Before we know it the sun will be up. I'll put more logs on the fire."

The woman pulled Will to her, her eyes shining in the firelight.

"Sleep beside me, tonight," she said. "Let me comfort you through this night as once you comforted me when I was afraid. "Be with me, tonight," she opened her arms to Will.

Will looked into the woman's eyes, and there he saw the kaleidoscope of Mary's life. Like a re-winding film, it showed images indelible in his memory, recollections of Mary's past, the small girl on the porch, on New Year day, the discovery of their love on her seventeenth birthday, the willow tree in the field of wildflowers and their transcendent spring day, Will saw the birth of Will Jr. and his and Mary's departure from their earthly existence.

Will fell to his knees, into Mary's embrace. He felt his mind fly into a dimension beyond human comprehension.

"I have loved you throughout eternity," Mary whispered.

Will Jr. woke from his sleep and snuggled into Will's and Mary's embrace.

"Papa! Mama!" he said, and went back to sleep.

Chapter Twenty Five

The Ghosts Never Go Away

The Vagabond

Maryland ~ Summer ~ 1865

Will sensed the gray light of early dawn on his closed eyelids and woke from a peaceful sleep. Mary, Will Jr., and Father Vollmer were gone. Will searched the campsite. Only the acrid aroma of charred logs remained to remind him of the day's early morning.

Will rushed to the intersecting road, but saw no sign of Father Vollmer's wagon. He stared at the road's interminable horizon and at the trackless clay and saw his footsteps chasing an unattainable illusion.

Next to the fire pit Will found a leather sack attached on either end by a slender strap with a pink ribbon tied loosely around the strap. Will removed the ribbon and placed it in the fold of Mother Vollmer's letter, and then he closed the lid. The inscription on its top flap read, "Vollmer Farm, Greenville, Georgia."

Will brushed his fingers over the sack's imprint. As he tried to bring back his memories the earth beneath the campsite rumbled and its shocks knocked Will to the ground. The earth fissured in long slithering cracks. Seeds of eon swirled in blinding winds and rain cascaded like hypnotic waterfalls from an open sky.

In an instant, the earth and sky calmed. Willows, sycamores and oaks, in the flower of their maturities, were restored as they had been designed by an unknown creative force.

Will slung the sack over his shoulder and started north, along the highway. Birds flew in their early morning rituals. The sun rose hot and the landscape came alive in sound and color. Inquisitive flowers on tall stems overlooked the highway's edge, a running stream sparkled in the woods and bright plants their stems crowded with pink and blue blooms floated on the stream's surface.

Will walked the highway as if he were out for an early morning stroll. He had experienced the power of everlasting love and its transcendental language careening between a rare feeling of serenity and a deep sense of loss.

From a curved side of the highway Will eased down a slope to a rock studded shelf and sat against its mossy wall. He stared into the distance his mind connected to its unfolding universe beyond the horizon. He drank in the sight of a glittering stream and the dazzling landscape c a r p e t e d before him. He saw a profusion of wildflowers of every imaginable color all dancing carelessly in cool puffs of air forming a colorful carpet along the stream's edge and beyond the stream, willow trees grew.

Will slid Mother Vollmer's letter out of his pocket and read it again. "Where are you, Mother?" Will called out. "Father, Mary, and Will, Jr. have come to me. Why haven't you come to me?" he called out, again, looking heavenward. "Why haven't you come to me?" he repeated, hearing only the echoes of his mind.

"Mind if I join ya', lad," a voice called to Will from the highway.

"Plenty of room."

A stout man, a cigar clenched between his teeth, slid down the slope.

"Been sitting here long?"

"Where did you come from?"

"I'm a vagabond, lad, a time traveler. What ya' been thinkin' about?"

"Nothin' much."

"Young fellas are always thinking about something," the vagabond winked. "Maybe that pretty lass back home."

"I'm just looking," Will said, sweeping his arm to the stream and field of wildflowers and pollinating butterflies, "and trying to find answers to questions that have no answers."

The vagabond blew a cloud of smoke into the air.

"It's a slice of paradise out there. The fluttering of all those butterflies sounds like a gentle rain. Indeed! A slice of paradise it is," he concluded.

"It reminds me of home."

"You'll get there, lad."

"I was about to have some bread, pleased to share with you."

"I need no food," the vagabond patted his stomach.

"Had a bad time in the war, lad?"

Will looked ahead to the field of wildflowers. He didn't answer.

"Well you don't have to answer."

"Not just the war," Will said.

"Bad times in war, an' what comes from war have a way of showing."

Will looked at the vagabond's twinkling blue eyes and fatherly smile.

"The ghosts never go away," Will said.

The vagabond exhaled a long puff of smoke. He flicked a burnt ash off his cigar and turned to Will.

"They might never go away, but ya' sure can control them."

"How?" Will retorted, skeptically.

"Here's how I see it, lad. Out there," he pointed his cigar, like a lecturer's pointer. "Out there, beyond the sun and the stars, in spaces we cannot see, and here on earth, we may never know is the universal soul of humankind."

"I don't know what you mean?"

"It's all around us, lad. It's infinite, forever. We are pieces of that soul. When our times come we split off and we are born to earth. People here and people past and people still to come are all parts of the universal soul; we are all tied together."

Will looked quizzically at the vagabond calmly blowing a stream of smoke rings into the air.

"It has always been there, lad," the vagabond continued. "It's the sky and the stars and the sun and the moon and the air we breathe. It is life's force. It's what makes us think and move, love and hate, live and die. And there are always opposites; can't have day without night, or joy without sadness or good without evil. I tell ya' lad," the vagabond patted Will's knee, "good pieces split off that soul all the time and they come to earth and they hold out their hands to help and they create good things for folks. Bad pieces also split off, and they cheat and oppress, and they put snares in our paths to make us feel sick and powerless. They come uninvited into our lives when we are low bringing with them unspeakable hardships. They lodge in our imaginations, toy with our minds, and keep us under their spells, if we let them. They are phantom tricksters from the dark side of the soul; they are chameleons who change colors for their own amusement and our discomfort."

"They are with me day and night? Will said, looking at the landscape before him, his mind affirming its beauty while contemplating his unremitting pain.

"Here's what I do," the vagabond said. "I take a deep breath, and then," he spit a brown stream over the stony ledge, "I spit in their smirking faces. I imagine I

133

have a big shoe on my foot and with my big imagined shoe, I boot 'em out of my mind."

"You imagine you have a big shoe and you boot 'em out with it," Will said with a rare audible chuckle.

"That's what I do, lad. I see that big shoe bootin' those demons out of my mind."

"And, it works?"

"Most of the time it works," he flicked an ash off his cigar. "There are times when those devils get madder than rabid dogs and they come snarlin' back. Then ya' know what I do?" he exhaled a cloud of smoke.

"Will looked at the vagabond, inquisitively, his lips curled in a slight smile.

"My imagination grows a bigger shoe and I boot 'em in their nether lands and send 'em squealing out of my mind into their dark corners.

"What do you mean?"

"How to put it, lad," the vagabond paused, "You're from Georgia, right?"

"How did you know that?"

"Let's just say I know a lot of things. What part of Georgia are you from?"

"Don't really know. I saw a map once. Looked like I lived near the middle, maybe a little south. I don't rightly know."

"You mean goin' to the lower part of the land?"

Will understood the vagabond's meaning and laughed. The vagabond removed his cigar and joined in the laughter. Within seconds Will and the vagabond laughed, lustily.

"There are times when too many of em' play with my mind and my imagination can't build a bigger shoe. That's when I call on the legions of good souls in my life, past and present. Those nibbling devils can't handle them. They know my army is more powerful than their tricks."

"I wish my path was clear," Will said.

"You'll find your way, lad," the vagabond patted Will's knee. "You may not know it now and you may not see it and you might not even think it, but somewhere along your way you'll fulfill many purposes. You need no monuments, lad; they are unfeeling stone that turn to dust when their memories dry up. Your monument is in the lives you will touch. Out there," he pointed with his cigar, "all is known and all is recorded."

"I hope you are right."

"Hope is a good thing, lad. Belief and hope is a more powerful combination."

Will looked at the vagabond and smiled. "A big foot in the nether land, you say."

"That's what I say," the vagabond shook his head, and repeated, "That's what I say," he smiled back, and then simultaneously they exploded in laughter.

"It's gettin' dark, and a storm's comin'," the vagabond said.

"Best be on my way to find shelter," Will said.

"Closest shelter hereabout is thirteen miles up the road, the Widow's Island; darnedest thing, a small island and a broken down footbridge poking out of the river. People swear it popped up out of nowhere. They say a widow is trapped on it and she can't get off it."

The vagabond climbed up the stony ledge and pulled Will up to the highway.

"Thirteen miles up the road you can't miss it."

"That's the northbound train, lad," the vagabond pointed to the sound of a distant whistle of an unseen train wafting over the treetops.

"Where am I now?" Will asked.

"You're in Mary-land, lad. Mary-land," he emphasized, "You came a long way."

Will walked a short distance, and then he stopped and looked back.

The vagabond was gone.

Chapter Twenty Six

Widow's Island

Prisoner of Despair

Maryland ~ Summer ~ 1865

Widow's Island came into Will's view from the highway overlooking the river channel. It was once accessible by a footbridge that lay broken in the river's lapping waters. Across the river on the ascending mountainside, trees, soft and green in daylight, glittered orange and gold as the sun went down.

Smoke curled languidly out of the pine cottage's stone chimney. Next to the barn a garden flourished, where the widow filled her wicker basket with its springtime offerings. She wore a faded purple dress that covered her from neck to ankle. Will thought the widow older than he, but not old, and taller than she appeared.

"I could use some shelter for the night!" he called out.

After a brief pause, the widow responded, in a spiritless voice.

"If you can get across, you're welcome to the barn," she answered.

The channel waters swelled in the gathering storm.

Lightning flashed in the blackening sky. Rolling thunder reverberated in Will's head; he felt hard rain slash his face. He went into the wet woods that hemmed the river bank where he arranged fallen logs into a crude footbridge.

Will dragged his footbridge to the edge of the channel, pushed it over its lip, climbed into the choppy waters and pushed it forward until it came to rest on the island. He slung his sack on his back and stepped onto the footbridge, to the island, now a ghostly outline in the raging storm.

A powerful blast of wind knocked Will to his knees. The swelling channel waters crashed over him and lightning and thunder in the sky re-ignited the demons of his wartime traumas.

"You have no claim on me!" Will cried out, into the flashing thunderous night.

Enraged by their repulsion Will's demons returned, bent on possessing his body and soul, buzzing in his head, spewing their venom into his mind.

"Get out of my life!" Will cried out, again as the rain-slicked footbridge bounced violently, and the roiling waters in the channel overflowed the island.

Will saw the widow silhouetted against the flashing sky coming through the rain. He struggled to get up, but powerful blasts of wind blew him down and his demons returned, more virulent than before.

"I am coming for you!" she called out, her voice drowning in the din of the thunderous storm.

As quickly as the widow appeared, she disappeared. The rocking footbridge shook Will, still trying to regain his balance, still trying to get up and get to the safety of the island.

In the pounding rain the vagabond reappeared.

"Call on the good souls in your life, lad," he said, and then, he was gone.

"Mother, help me!" Will cried out.

The widow struggled through the rain-swept blackness buffeted by powerful blasts of wind, and got to the channel's edge.

"Take my hand!" she reached for Will, "Take my hand!" she cried out, a n d then disappeared into the raging channel waters.

Will crawled along the footbridge to the channel's edge. He reached in and pulled the widow out of the water, onto the island. In those moments Will knew he had been guided to the island for a purpose greater than himself.

Together, Will and the widow waded through the flooded island to the safety of the cottage. In the flashing night, Will discerned the widow's features. He saw her haunted dark eyes, her face etched in her life's pain, and yet, undefeated.

In the night, wind and rain beat relentlessly, rattling the cottage, deluging the already flooded island. Lighting strikes burst age-old trees across the river into orange flames consuming the ascending mountainside.

In the cottage, Will shivered in the blanket that covered his nakedness. He had won his battle with his demons on the footbridge, but they returned, resurrecting his fears.

Will shut his eyes to deny their existence, but they assaulted him with a ferocity his imagery could no longer contain. He saw his room filled with comrades, staring at him through expressionless eyes. Will got up and ran to the widow.

In the somber glow of her lamp, the widow sat on the edge of her bed drying her wet black hair that lay limp on her shoulders.

Streaks of lightning and cracks of thunder ripped into Will's mind. He stood immobilized in the widow's doorway. She looked at Will, still shuddering at the re-emergence of his traumatic memories.

And then, the widow opened her arms.

"Come to me," she said, softly, and Will ran into the safety of her embrace.

"I have been a prisoner on this island. You have freed me, my son." In the twilight of his awareness quiet tears streamed down Will's face.

"I can continue my search to find my lost baby girl, your sister, the innocent we never knew. The firmament is endless, but I will find her. In another time, and in another place, the light of life will shine in her eyes, and then my mission will be complete. Sleep, my son, the ghosts are quiet, now," Mother Vollmer, said, kissing Will's face.

The new day dawned bright and clear. The garden next to the barn blazed in bright colors. The placid river and channel waters ran smooth and lazy. The trees on the mountainside were lush and green and the footbridge defied the unsettled night and remained intact.

A rain dove pecked at the window and with a slow fluttering of its wings, it flew away.

On the window sill a music box played; its figurines spun around, and Will remembered. He put the music box in his sack and looked back, once more, into the cottage's surreal quiet.

As he crossed on the footbridge Will knew he was following Mother Vollmer's spirit off the island. He climbed up the stony path to the highway, from which he heard a groaning noise in the river.

The island was sinking.

The footbridge washed away. The barn and garden drowned, and the pine cottage swept away in the rising river waters.

The river dimpled wide and deep over the submerged island, and from prehistoric trenches water foamed on the sunlit surface that covered its watery grave.

The island was gone.

Mother Vollmer was free.

Will resumed his northbound journey.

Chapter Twenty Seven

The Messenger

My Heart is an Empty Vessel

Maryland ~ Summer ~ 1865

Will remembered the forgotten highway and Widow's Island. They were forever sealed in his memory. He realized the comfort both brought him and the glimpse into a world that only few living mortals had been privileged to see.

The day was clear and warm. Will had no idea of his ultimate destination. His intuition told him his path had been foreordained. He walked on a north road that ran along the straight reach of a river.

To the west, willow trees lined a stream. Beyond the stream a surly mountain angled down and along its wide corner ran a ribbon of railroad tracks. A steam engine rounded the mountain tugging a coal-laden tender and a train of worn boxcars.

The steam engine belched plumes of smoke like a flag in the wind. Will sprinted across the road past the willow trees, splashing through the stream and racing along sooty tracks. He grabbed the door frame of an open boxcar and pulled himself up.

Inside he eyed a shadowy figure coming toward him.

"A railroad detective," he thought.

142

"I'll be roughed up and thrown off the train."

The figure that Will saw was the spectral Union soldier; he watched with widened eyes as he held his balance in the rocking boxcar.

In the light, the soldier came into sharper focus. He was transformed; his eyes were bright, his skin glowed and his personality was quick.

"Mind if I sit to your side?" he asked.

Will nodded yes.

The soldier rested his back against the boxcar's vibrating wall. He and Will sat side-by-side, both captivated by the train's hypnotic motion. Burdened by an broken promise and troubled by unresolved guilt, the soldier broke the silence.

"I didn't die that day I saw you in the woods," he confessed. "A few days after that night on your farm, I died in a cornfield. The rifle fire was so fierce it cut the cornstalks to the ground. Since that day I searched for you, to seek your forgiveness and to learn my broken promise to your mother was somehow fulfilled and you received her letter, the letter you now guard in your sack."

The soldier stared out the open door mesmerized by the running landscape, his thoughts flowing to Will.

"As I lay in the cornfield I looked up to the sky, with fading eyes," he said. "A soldier knelt beside me. I handed him your mother's letter. He took it from my trembling hand. I couldn't speak, but he sensed my wishes and rose to his feet.

The soldier pulled me into a world of magnificent gardens and reflecting pools. I learned the infinite mind of the universe, that my soul is immortal and my life eternal. I discovered love is the foundation of mortal existence. My life is recorded in a cosmic library where I can relive my past and atone for the wrongs I committed during my earthly existence, like the wrong I did your father."

The two men rocked involuntarily to the train's jolting rhythm. Then the soldier turned to Will who sat pensively, processing the strange thoughts he had telepathically received from the soldier.

"What do you wish for?" the soldier asked.

"To relive a day in my life," Will answered.

"I'm not sure what happened. I'll never forget that day. It was perfect and best of all was the feel of Mary's hand in mine. We ran through a field of wildflowers, to a knoll, where a giant willow tree stood, beside a sparkling stream lined on both sides with flowers of all colors. Mary and I made love in the heart of the willow tree. I had this feeling I was living only in those moments."

Will paused.

"I felt as if I had no past, no future, only those wonderful moments. I would give anything to relive that day, but now, my heart is a broken vessel."

Will pulled his sack tight against his chest and withdrew into himself.

"Can a broken heart be fixed?" he asked.

"The pieces of a broken vessel can be sealed together," the soldier, said. "It will look whole. It will function, as it was intended to function. But always it will be fragile and bear the scars that are memories of its loss. The same is true of the human heart. Your memories will sustain you. At the same time, they will bedevil you, because you desire to make them real. Where I am hearts become whole, again. One day, your heart will be made whole."

"What news do you bring me?" Will asked.

"My search for your father was successful. We walked in the peach orchard where I begged his forgiveness, which he generously granted me. Your father and mother and their lost baby girl are now together, reunited for all eternity in a place where there is always peace and tranquility," the soldier telepathically transmitted his news.

"What of my Mary and our son?" Will questioned as the train sped into a dark tunnel.

When it emerged into the light of day, the spectral soldier was gone."

Chapter Twenty Eight

Take My Hand

Greenville Railroad Yard ~ New Jersey

Early Morning ~ New Year Day ~ 1900

The shack inside was as black as the snowy night outside was white. Will heard the mournful whistle of an inbound train. He thought he was dreaming and then he heard it again. Will lit his lantern and went to the shack's frosted window. The frozen floor shocked his bare feet. He looked through the fogged window at a steam engine, tugging a boxcar past the shack, and then it disappeared into a cloud of swirling snow.

Will dressed and left the shack to complete his tour of the yard. He pushed through snow-choked corridors of sullen boxcars hoping not to discover frozen dead bodies as he had so many times in years past. He banged on snow-caked doors and jiggled frozen locks until his gloves froze to his hands.

Spasms deep within his chest throttled Will until his entire being screamed for relief. Despite the freezing night Will burned hotter than the hottest summer day in Georgia and hotter than the bricks heating on his potbelly stove.

"I look like a polar bear, Mary," Will whispered, hoarsely, plowing his way through snow drifts.

146

"You read about polar bears in the books father bought for you; you were so smart, I never knew what you saw in a simple farm boy," Will made light of his distress.

"The snowflakes are like silver dollars. Nights like this make me feel we are forever."

Will held up his lantern to a luminous white light shining through the falling snow. He pressed and then opened his eyes to an ethereally beautiful woman coming to him, holding out her hand. Will reached for her, but before they touched, the woman disappeared.

A sense of peace enveloped Will. He raised his face to the falling snow; he felt reborn. Will didn't feel the lantern slip from his hand. He thought the willow tree that had watched over him through his long lonely years looked regal in its white coat. Then, he saw the willow turn a rich summer's green, and suddenly, the willow seemed far away. Will closed his eyes and slumped into the snow his lantern glowing through its frosted windows.

"I've come for you, Will," the voice was indescribably gentle.

"I came to you long ago, when we were very young; now, I've come to you, to take you home."

Will opened, and then closed his eyes.

"The peach orchard is in bloom, it fulfills its promise of rebirth. Mother and father and your long lost sister await you, and Will, Jr. is excited to see his father. Take my hand, Will; when you touch my hand, you will know."

"Mary," Will's voice faltered.

"Yes, Will, take my hand. I've come to take you home."

When their hands touched, the anguish of Will's life dissolved. In an instant, he was in a field of wildflowers. At the top of gentle rise a willow tree sang in gentle breezes. A boy broke loose from his mother and ran down the slope, laughing. His mother ran after him. The boy leaped into Will's outstretched arms. Will held him tight, and then the boy wriggled away, running happily through the field swinging at wildflowers.

Will and Mary met in the shade of their willow tree, she was eternally beautiful, and Will was in the flower of his youth. Mary handed Will the soldier boy doll she had with her when a small girl, on New Year day in 1850.

"You kept it with you all this time."

"It has been a difficult journey for you," Mary said.

Tears welled in Will's eyes.

'Now you are home," Mary smiled.

Chapter Twenty Nine

There Are No Coincidences

Greenville Railroad Yard ~ New Jersey

Jersey

Summer ~ 1945

A cathedral-like quiet filled the musty shack. I returned Mother Vollmer's letter to its desiccated envelope. I looked, again, at the few remaining possessions of Will's life.

I felt like an intruder. In a strange way I believe resurrecting parts of Will's life, touching what he had touched throughout his lonely years would meet with his approval. My thoughts deepened. I felt Will's presence. I am convinced a human life is not the sum of a handful of objects. The pink ribbon I smoothed between my fingers meant more to Will than a simple strand of silk.

I wound the spring of Will's music box to hear the music he once heard; it didn't play, its figurines stood immobile on its turntable. I looked at Will's sketch of him and Mary. I examined their carefree smiles and the obvious love they shared. I don't believe their lives extinguished like burned out filaments in a light bulb.

I don't know if it mattered that I was in Will's room where he spent most of his life. I am sure Will was more than just a name in a crumbling letter I found among his scant possessions, undiscovered for almost fifty years.

Why did I find Will's letter? I know the ghosts of war that stalked Will; they hound me, too. Will and I might be bound by the threads of a universal soul. Another of life's mysteries that one day faith and science might unravel.

Will's sketch was haunting. I looked at their smiles, and their laughing eyes and their cheek-to-cheek caress, and the imposing willow tree and the sparkling stream, behind. The intensity was so sharp I felt I was in the full life of the picture.

Why are you laughing? Did you splash through the stream? Did you pick wildflowers on your way home? I asked. Beyond the joy I saw in their faces I had no right to their private moments.

Then I heard a voice, but I saw no one.

I heard the voice, again.

"Do not forget me." I flashed back to the chapel in Italy, to the German soldier, and the letter to his wife and the picture he had painted.

I took his picture from my wallet and placed it next to Will's sketch. But for the differences in time, languages and color the pictures were identical, as were their inscriptions.

Will and Mary, Our Secret Place, 1863, and *Wilhelm und Maria, Unser Geheimer Ort, 1943*."

The soldier and his wife were in the shack, bathed in a white beam of light, holding hands.

"Your promise is kept; my letter has been delivered," the soldier said.

I thought about the letter I never sent to the girl I had fallen in love with. I never forgot her. She was always on my mind. I dreamed she would be waiting for me when I came home. I know she got me through the rough times. I hoped she would be on the pier. I wish I could see her now, and tell her I love her and take the chance she would say she loves me, too.

The soldier and his wife didn't speak.

Since that day in the chapel I kept the guilt I felt bottled within me. I sensed the soldier and his wife were thinking I was the guy who stole their future.

"I was only trying to survive," I said, apologetically.

"We were soldiers, then," the soldier responded.

I nodded.

"When you touched my letter to my wife, you had a recrimination you wouldn't acknowledge."

"What are you talking about?"

"The letter you never sent."

"What do you know about that letter?"

"I know you regretted never sending it to the girl you had fallen in love with."

I thought I was hallucinating.

"As I drifted away," the soldier said, "I found myself in the vestibule of my unconscious mind, the portal to the infinite mind of humanity. I had access to many things; one of them was knowledge of the treasured box you kept under your bed. In the instant you touched my letter to my wife I knew you were remorseful at not having sent your letter to the woman you love. I carried out that mission for you."

I thought it strange an enemy soldier I killed in a chapel in Italy had become my romantic match-maker.

He and his wife were still in the shack. I thanked him for doing what I should have done. They smiled, and then, hand-in-hand they walked into the beam of white light that brought them to me.

For a long time I groped for explanations; that's when I heard a knock on the open door.

A young woman stood in the full light that illuminated the room, her presence broke my distraction.

"I'll be working here for the summer."

I went to greet her.

"It has been a long time, Will. I have worried for you, and now, you are home."

She pressed my letter into the palm of my hand.

"I knew it would bring us together," she said, softly.

"I dreamed of this day, Mary."

"As have I, Will."

In that moment, the music box played, its melody filled the room, its figurines danced, and outside, snowflakes flurried in the sun.

ATTRIBUTIONS

Page 66

Home, Sweet Home
A song sung by Confederate and Union soldiers
Composed by John Howard Payne

Just before the Battle, Mother
A song sung by Confederate and Union Soldiers
Composed by George Root